AF392374

Axel Flame

The Eye of Amrok

Rafa Garza

EDIQUID

AXEL FLAME
The Eye of Amrok
© Rafa Garza

Edited by: Corporación Ígneo, S.A.C.
For its editorial seal Ediquid
José Olaya 169, Ofic. 504, Miraflores. Lima, Perú
First edition, may, 2025

ISBN: 978-956-6404-62-0

www.grupoigneo.com
Email: contacto@grupoigneo.com | Phone number: +51 955 071 270
Facebook: Grupo Ígneo | X: @editorialigneo | Instagram: @grupoigneo

Collection: Nuevas Voces

Contents

Preface

In both the vast expanse of the universe and the realms beyond, everything has a beginning —a genesis that unfolds even in the stillness where time halts and eternity becomes the recess of the Creators. It is precisely in that recess that the story commences— a tale destined to echo through the corridors of time. For, much like time itself, the story is boundless. Yet the historical cycles it begets are finite; hence, cycles commence and conclude, and all within them rise and crumble like a house of cards.

Legend speaks of the Creators, who, weary of meticulously counting the grains of sand stored in eternity, birthed universes. Within these universes, they breathed life into galaxies, stars, and worlds. Life that is bestowed upon the seemingly lifeless —whether worms that devour rocks or sentient beings— all conceived out of sheer boredom, and they observed.

To enhance their amusement, the Creators fashioned diverse beings with unique abilities, entire races, and civilizations. Astonishing abilities that defied the very laws of the universe are granted, and among them are those without bounds, shaped to mold everything around them like clay in the hands of a child.

Thus emerged Medrian, the inaugural planet in our universe, seemingly out of nothingness. Amrok, one of the Creators, bestowed sentience upon its first inhabitants. He colored their bones with the hues of the universe and adorned their heads with a wet layer of algae to keep them moist.

Amrok lived among them, nurturing, guiding, and developing them until weariness set in. He imparted to them a language —the language of the Creators— and the art of living and surviving through time. But, like every cycle, a day arrived when Medrian wearied of its evolution. It was precisely at that moment when walking became more tedious than sitting. Following the customary Creator fashion, Amrok could not endure the tedium and decided to depart in search of another grand idea or the creation of a new universe, leaving behind his initial creations.

Before departing, Amrok, the youthful Creator, committed the unthinkable —audacious and mischievous, characteristic of a Creator despite their ageless nature. He selected one of his living, thinking creations, with skin as dark as the universe and seaweed-like hair, and bestowed upon them a wondrous gift.

Among all in that world, he chose Kendorf, an orphan of Medrian who had spent a lifetime caring for his younger brother, Zetkorf. Amrok gifted him an eye in the form of a star. The star radiated with a brilliance akin to diamonds, indestructible and imbued with boundless power, containing a fragment of the life force of the Creator of universes.

Kendorf transcended into one of them —a Creator. Upon touching the star eye, he became immortal, a manipulator of time, a producer of stars, a progenitor of worlds and galaxies, omnipotent. Thus, a God was born, entrusted with the duty of safeguarding the inhabitants and turning Medrian into a paradise —a task he executed meticulously.

Until one day, Kendorf observed the unrelenting cycle of life around him —birth, growth, and death. He witnessed his brother Zetkorf aging, and though the elderly were revered for their wisdom, they also elicited pity, like a dying animal in the street, hungry and inching closer to death each day. And so, Kendorf watched as all those around him succumbed to death, creating sorrow in his heart and solitude in his soul. Loneliness felt akin to being alone in empty rooms, with vast walls and cold floors. The notion of abandonment assailed him, reminiscent of the abandonment he had endured when he had neither father nor mother.

And so, Kendorf did what any brother would do in his stead: he granted eternal life to his brother, Zetkorf. Upon defying death and the laws of the cycle, Zetkorf sought even greater power. He convinced himself that living forever was his destiny, but he aspired to become a God. It was then that he beseeched Kendorf, as a gift, for the knowledge of the universe —as if a man could bear the weight of the world on his shoulders. Although his loving brother did not deny the request and bestowed upon him eternal wisdom —the gift that solely emanated from Amrok's star.

Centuries passed, and Kendorf, much like Amrok, could not endure the monotony. His uncertainties about the rest of the universe expanded through time; his ideas and curiosity consumed his thoughts, as he spent entire days questioning the star about what existed before existence, what lies beyond the endless cosmos, and where the infinite ends and begins.

In Medrian, only Kendorf and Zetkorf pondered such questions, for on the planet, peace reigned with sustenance for all, though tragedies existed they are erased by the passage of time.

One day, the bearer of the star —the newly born Eternal, Kendorf— decided to depart in search of Amrok or any other Creator who could help dispel his doubts and explore the vast universe crafted by the one who no longer possessed an eye. In his farewell, he bestowed upon his brother the power to rule the planet, proclaiming it before all its inhabitants. With his infinite power, he ascended into the sky, placing his image before all subjects, then vanished into the darkness of the universe, akin to the color of his skin.

Zetkorf, holder of eternal knowledge and an unending yet powerless life, felt betrayed by his brother, who abandoned him without bestowing more power, leaving him in pursuit of answers to the same doubts.

Nevertheless, with knowledge came awakening for the new king, as when the sun rises and dispels the naive night. This awakening allowed Zetkorf to craft his own plan, for now, he understood the laws of the eternal —those that narrate a beginning of everything and a cycle that has an end, leading to another cycle. This was how Kendorf's brother interpreted it. For him, the concept of a beginning was devoid of meaning, for nothing can commence if there hasn't been something before.

Therefore, for something to begin, there must be an end. Just as all that is good stems from something bad and what exists as energy must have a counterpart, Amrok himself must have an opposing Creator. Thus, the star, brimming with power, should necessarily have a counterpart.

This was how Zetkorf, the new king, embarked on the quest for the origin in a different form. Throughout Kendorf's absence, his brother sought a Dark Star, one endowed with infinite power but opposing his brother's. The planet turned black, delving into excavations, teaching its inhabitants to mix components and experiment with alchemical potions.

These concoctions served as nourishment for the Creators and remedies for ailments, but some were crafted for darker purposes. Indiscriminately, he burned all that lived, for what he sought did not dwell in the realm of the living but in the dead. Yet, he found no success. No matter how he searched, he could not uncover that eye residing beneath or parallel to Amrok's eye-turned-star.

Then, the immortal king returned from his journey. Kendorf arrived as he had departed —empty-handed and brimming with doubts. This affected his mood; disheartened, disillusioned, and profoundly sad, he secluded himself in his palace for five years, which, given his eternity, passed in the blink of an eye.

During this time, Zetkorf, blinded by ambition for power, set about recruiting subjects. He chose the best to initiate a revolution against his brother and seize the star. The day arrived, and the younger of the two orphaned brothers entered the room of the older, though not in appearance, certainly in years.

"Tell me, brother, what can I do for you?"

"Brother... Your Majesty," replied Zetkorf and continued, "I believe the time has come for you to surrender the entire kingdom. Your fortress has crumbled, as has your spirit, and your vigor to rule no longer exists."

"Zetkorf, I have witnessed what you are capable of and believe, in my heart, that you can become a great leader for Medrian," Kendorf responded with sincere words and continued, "However, I have also seen what you have done and what you have become. During these five years since my return, I have remained on the sidelines to observe your reaction, and all I have witnessed is how you conspire against me. In your ambition for power, you bring the planet down with you. But I do not entirely blame you, for the inhabitants allowed themselves to be swayed by your spirit, sustaining your hope."

Zetkorf kept his distance, for his brother was aware of his conspiracy, and an attack would be futile; Kendorf would obliterate them all, including him.

"Still, my brother, I venerate you, and from the depths of my heart, I shall make a confession. In my journey through the infinite cosmos, and of the universes crafted by Amrok, I have discovered other worlds, and in them, I have witnessed life, brother. There are three, besides Medrian, making a total of four, and in all of them, Amrok's hand is unmistakable. There are beings like you and me, but different in appearance.

With the power of the star, I have donned their skins and observed as they contemplate their planets, gazing at the constellations from afar. So, like you, I have sought the other eye of the Creator of universes, but luck has eluded me. I believe no Creator would relish lacking vision, though they don't require it to dwell in what exists beyond existence."

Then, Kendorf paused and stood beside his brother, right at the edge of a colossal window adorning the castle they inhabited.

"After reflecting for this time, I have comprehended Amrok's plan and why he bestowed the star upon me from the outset. It is not my destiny to rule the planets of this universe or any other, but to discover them and allow future generations to unite civilizations and, thereby, the planets that harbor life."

"What do you mean?" asked Zetkorf, suspecting that something ominous would follow his brother's next words.

"So, brother, I have decided that my time has come. Now, I understand that this is the only way to reunite with Amrok and those who sit by his side in the eternal space."

"Kendorf, I understand what you're saying, and I solemnly promise to seek the unity of the planets after you hand over the star."

"No, Zetkorf, I have decided, and I have heard Amrok's intent. It will not be me who hands over the star," replied Kendorf, floating away from the window with the star, crystalline and harder than a diamond, pulsating with energy.

"The star and, therefore, the Creator of universes, Amrok, will decide who should bear it and be its guardian."

This silenced Zetkorf and shifted his mood. He couldn't believe what he was hearing, and despite resisting the idea, he couldn't attack; it would destroy him.

"The Eye of Amrok will choose an inhabitant from the four planets, who will reign for fifty years in this universe and all that resides within it. During this cycle, the star will select two inhabitants from each planet, anointing them with a touch of its infinite power. When these reach the age of fifteen, the star will choose a single planet, and its two selected inhabitants will compete to protect it. It will not be a violent competition but one of cunning and wisdom."

And so, Zetkorf inquired:

"But what will happen if the star falls into the hands of a dweller who is not its chosen one, and they pick it up? Have you not considered that?"

"Certainly, brother. In such a case, they may wield it, but ultimately, the star will always return to its rightful owner. After fifty years of reign, the star's possessor will live only another fifty years, as a reward or punishment for their performance."

Kendorf's body began to radiate light as he remained suspended, and from it emerged a brilliance so intense that it banished the planet from darkness for a few seconds. Then, this light transformed into a streak heading into the deep universe, disappearing from Zetkorf's view and from all the inhabitants of Medrian, the first planet.

Chapter I

Barely fourteen years after writing for a local newspaper and publishing on her blog about the surprising disappearance of a father and his son, Amanda Ríos sat at her computer in her small apartment in New York. She observed the similarities in another case that occurred on the same date, over 5,000 miles away in Turkey.

In both instances, there was a sudden excursion outside their respective homes; the father cradled the newborn in his arms, mourning the loss of the mother during childbirth. Attendees, with bittersweet expressions, celebrated life while bidding farewell, shedding tears to death —an inevitability for any being created and governed by the laws of the universe.

She watched them walk into the dark night and vanish into it. There was no trace of abduction; no one had demanded a ransom or claimed their belongings. The police, as is customary in such cases, investigated after forty-eight hours, and the cases remained open as Amanda read about them.

The journalist and blogger, better known as Ammy in the cyber world, hadn't wasted any time. Over these fourteen years, she devoted countless hours to attempting, through social media, organizations, contacts, and every means at her disposal, to uncover a clue revealing the whereabouts of the young widowed father, remembered by neighbors as "John Flame," an unremarkable carpenter who worked wood like no other, crafting furniture resembling artistic paintings or ancient marble sculptures. Yet, she had achieved nothing. After all, that wasn't her sole occupation; she also had to keep the newspaper notes and her blog, *AmmyNews.com*, updated to survive and put food and drink on her table.

That night brought back many memories, especially on the fourteenth anniversary of her first journalistic note and the disillusionment of the proper follow-up to the cases. Watching how news articles sink into a deep, earthy cycle where they are replaced by others and in turn by others; as news happens daily, and the past is a place where only lovers dwell because they remember and fall in love again. But normal people, those who breathe smoke on the streets, always need fresh and new information to start their day.

Thus, nostalgia invaded her, and while clicking through the articles on her blog, she found a comment on that note referring to a similar case and attaching the link to the publication. In the past, she had overlooked it, or perhaps, upon opening it, she had realized she didn't understand what was written because it was in another language, and symbols representing a letter in one language are cursed in another and revered in the next.

Besides, there was no online translator back then, but now things were different. The note appeared in English, the language she mastered in addition to Latin American Spanish; the latter by heritage, not academic formation like the former.

The note narrated in great detail the similarities of the disappearance: the open space closed to view as it was nighttime —darkness hides from the eyes of man— the matriarchal loss, and the absence of posthumous traces. Amanda read all of this while savoring a Cinco Grados black coffee in a porcelain cup with the logo of the local baseball team, to which she was a fan.

The night fall arrived surprising her, with sleep lacking because the dark and bitter nectar of coffee is it enemy. Suddenly, the silence shattered, and from the main door came the sounds of knuckles hitting the wood, reverberating on all the sheetrock walls, creating a thunderous echo that unnerved her, causing her to drop the porcelain cup. It crashed to the floor, shattering into hundreds of pieces with the New York Yankees logo, the noise it made joining the sound of the knuckles on the door

—like the cheer of fans attending the stadium and witnessing their team's victory.

Ammy tried to calm her nerves by breathing slowly and responded to the knocking on the door, as everyone does when they are far from it and have to get up from their seat, where they were perfectly comfortable. When she reached the door, she peeked through the peephole, but the desperate figure on the other side was unrecognizable. She asked for the person's name, and he replied, "John Flame." Amanda was left speechless.

She first unlocked the latch and then turned the doorknob that separated them. As soon as the door opened, the widowed father entered, accompanied by a restless-haired teenage boy. John wore jeans with a colorless polo shirt and a cap with the local team's logo; seemingly senseless to wear in the darkness as the visor is useless against the moon, which blankets the Earth in white.

The young boy with restless hair was covered in a long coat down to his ankles and long-sleeved, darker than the night itself —even the most experienced cat wouldn't see him if he passed by with light feet. Immediately after rushing in, they closed the door, and John spoke with anguished words.

"I don't have much time. I read about you," the widowed father spoke while nervously scanning the door. "This is my son, Axel, the same one who disappeared with me fourteen years ago. He'll explain. Please take care of him, as the other one wasn't as fortunate and won't return freely."

After this, John, who had once disappeared, did it again —but now of his own free will. He left through the same door that had opened and closed before, disappearing once again into the darkness of the New York suburbs, this time alone. His unfortunate son, who had lost his mother during childbirth, now watched his father run as the door closed slowly. The astonished eyes of the blogger, torn between watching each of them, locked onto Axel's, and both stood petrified in the silence that followed the click of the door bolt.

Amanda observed Axel's deeply bronzed face, as if he had been exposed to the sun for fourteen years. Anxious to break the awkward silence that arises when two strangers stand side by side, staring directly into each other's eyes, she tried to articulate a sentence. Several thoughts crossed her mind: *How are you? Would you like something to eat? Nice to meet you!* She even considered introducing herself in her mind. However, before she could utter a word, Axel interrupted her, like halting the sun with a foot just as it intends to rise at dawn.

"I understand you have many questions, Miss Ríos, but it's necessary that we leave this place immediately. My father is sure they were tracking him, investigating every place he stopped for more than a minute, so please gather your things as quickly as possible. They won't be long."

The bronzed-skinned youth spoke without raising his voice or panic in his words, knowing that only his father had a Knolot tracker. Axel's had been removed before escaping from that planet.

Ammy, the blogger, paid no attention to the words of the young man who had disappeared fourteen years ago and walked toward the living room, where her computer was. Thinking of sitting down and asking Axel questions about his disappearance, he followed her without taking his eyes off the door through which they had entered. Amanda Ríos sat in her black leather recliner, ready to write.

"How about we calm down a bit first, and then you can tell me where you've been all this time?" she said, speaking like the seasoned reporter she was, using her skill in the art of interviewing.

But a loud noise in the exterior hallway interrupted her, changing her mood.

"It's them; we have to get out of here," Axel said, signaling for silence with his right hand, placing his index finger on his lips, urging them to move as stealthily as possible toward an alternative exit.

Amanda pointed to the side window leading to the emergency stairs, and as they walked toward it, the reporter grabbed her bag and Axel's hand. When they opened the window silently, like a diamond thief in a jewelry store, Axel climbed out first, then extended his hand to the reporter. She followed, recalling similar situations while chasing exclusives in celebrity cases.

Outside the apartment, the restless-haired young man made the same hush sign, holding her waist with one arm. Together, they let themselves drop from the eighth floor, where Ammy's apartment was. She stifled a scream, muffled by Axel's hand.

Falling like a rock from the lofty Pizza Tower, the two bodies remained connected by the bronzed-skinned young man's slender arms. However, the landing was as gentle as a feather on a mattress, agile as a stray cat. Axel released Ammy, who, still in shock, dropped to her knees. She couldn't believe what had just happened, even though she had seen it with her own eyes.

From her vantage point on the ground, she noticed something under Axel's coat as it billowed in the wind. Where his feet connected to his legs through bony ankles, lines of bright blue glowed, running all the way up his legs to his waist. She only managed to glimpse up to his knee before Axel adjusted the coat.

"What is that?" asked the eager reporter, her curiosity piqued.

"A long story. I'll tell you when we're safe," replied Axel, the one with glowing blue lines on his legs. He stretched out his hand and took hers, pulling her to her feet.

They began to walk toward a nearby crowd of people gathered around food stalls, bars, and nightlife venues, all buzzing with young revelers gearing up to start the night.

Chapter II

When those fleeing arrived at a café famous for its fresh doughnuts and Cinco Grados coffee imported from the world's most exclusive plantations, Amanda chose a seat by the window that provided a view of her apartment. The young man with restless hair sat beside her. Both watched the danger from afar, like fearful, hungry mice catching the scent of cheese from a distance, anxious to know what was happening.

Amanda ordered a double espresso and one of the café's famous glazed doughnuts. For Axel, who had fallen silent when questioned by the waitress, she ordered a chocolate milk and a couple of the same doughnuts, knowing they were the café's most renowned treat.

As the waitress walked away, Ammy fixed her piercing reporter's eyes on Axel and didn't hold back her words.

"Now you will tell me what I need to know. I followed you here, but speak honestly, or my credibility will waver, and I'll leave you alone, even if it goes against your father's request. I know neither of you more than by myths and my own words that once described you in a local newspaper."

Her clever persistence was met with calm anticipation. Axel, who had expected her barrage of questions, nodded and answered without hesitation.

"Where have you been all this time?" she asked.

"I'll answer your questions because you trusted me enough to follow me here. But what I tell you may sound nonsensical, especially to someone as cultured as yourself, an experienced reporter. Still, I beg you to keep an open mind and not leave the table until I've said all I need to say, even if your questions are answered first," Axel replied solemnly.

Amanda, intrigued, agreed to listen.

"My father and I were taken to another planet, a very distant one where the inhabitants don't move their arms but do everything with their thoughts. They transport themselves swiftly from one place to another. I grew up in an isolated place, enclosed from all sides, where they taught me to speak properly and walk—all in what would be mere minutes of your day. Then my father came for me, forcibly taking me from that beautiful place and bringing me to another, buried beneath modernity."

"Wait, what do you mean by 'minutes of your day'?" Amanda interrupted.

"Upon arriving on this planet, my father explained that here, time moves much faster —days and years pass quickly. But on the planet, we were taken to, time is measured only in years, and those years are far longer than those on Earth," Axel explained.

Amanda, incredulous, eyed him skeptically but continued asking questions, doubting his psychological integrity.

"Alright, suppose I believe you. How did you return? And what are those blue lines on your legs?"

"We returned the same way we left—with the help of the swift ships built in Knolot. As for the blue lines, they are 'enhancers.' The inhabitants of that planet placed them on me after removing the tracker that had rendered my legs immobile."

Still doubtful, Amanda pressed on.

"You mentioned Knolot and its inhabitants chasing you. Why haven't you let me see them? I want to know who they are and what they look like."

"I understand your disbelief, Amanda Ríos, which is why I won't insist that you believe me. But if you wish to see them, there's no need to wait —they're already here. According to my father, the world will know of them any moment now. As for us, we only have to wait one more Earth year for the Eye of Amrok to decide which planet it will fall on. When it does, Perfidius

—the cruel king ruling now, a thief from Medrian— will leave us alone."

Axel's words left Amanda even more confused as she sipped her espresso and nibbled on the glazed doughnut.

Suddenly, the café cashier called for silence —a contradiction, as his loud voice commanded others to be quiet. The customers obeyed out of respect, and the televisions hanging around the café were turned up. All eyes fixed on the screens.

The live images being broadcast resembled scenes from history channels depicting the end of World War II. Giant mushroom clouds spread across the sky, destroying cities. But this time, it wasn't history —it was happening now.

"We confirm the disappearance of Los Angeles after a nuclear explosion," announced a broadcaster. Glances among the café's patrons intertwined as another commentator joined the broadcast, describing with terror the formation of a nuclear mushroom over Beijing and another over Moscow.

"We corroborate the simultaneous attack on the capitals of China and Russia," the somber voice continued.

An Arabic correspondent reported the fall of Baghdad, but his words were lost amid the café's customers, who only watched the images, their faces soaked with tears, tributaries overflowing down their cheeks.

"New attack reported in London, the capital of England," another journalist stated, his voice trembling. The news spread worldwide wherever electricity still sustained the live broadcast. After London, no new reports came, only palpable panic surrounding the attacked cities. Speculations ran wild —terrorists, rebels, major powers. Some even predicted the biblical apocalypse, though these claims drew less attention; there were no divine signs, only death and despair.

"It's them," Axel murmured under his breath. To his surprise, Ammy heard him, even as tears streamed down her face, mixing with the bitter taste of fear and disbelief.

Chapter III

On the other side of the country, in Washington, the capital of the modern world, the president and his cabinet —elite advisors— glided through the halls of the White House toward the underground bunker. Before ensuring their own safety, they secured the well-being of their families, confining them in another underground fortress equipped with every comfort and capable of housing a thousand souls. In this war of man, not only politicians held crucial positions but also families, a source of strength and sustenance for the soul.

As they locked themselves in, leaders of other countries replicated the same act. The head did not fall in the war of man; instead, the feet were the first to fight, for the brain held reason, and the heart, hope. Everyone received real-time reports of the unfolding chaos. Citizens took refuge in their homes; some looted stores and supermarkets as panic prevailed —an evil counselor for humanity. Dust and ash clouds expanded, enveloping more cities, feeding hysteria, and generating weeping and screams in their wake.

Those in charge of the war prepared for a counterattack: men and women of all ages and ranks, bound by the discipline that guides battles. Soldiers from all nations, even those not directly affected, polished their weapons and readied missiles capable of obliterating cities and civilizations. Powerful, swift planes roared through the skies like peacemakers concluding endless wars. Everyone waited, expectant.

Commanders-in-chief, generals, and secretaries, surrounded by vital information for informed decisions, hesitated to point fingers at the guilty. In this global disaster, responsibility lay with everyone. The U.S. president gave the green light, and missiles were aimed at the other continent.

North Korea and Iran were suspects —longstanding enemies— but the attacks on China and Russia, supposed allies, created contradictions. Still, suspicion fell upon them. Blame was necessary to reassure the people, and these nations, aware of the accusations, prepared their defenses and counterattacks to avoid incrimination.

Television screens, as some signals flickered intermittently while others held steady, showed world leaders distancing themselves from atrocities, calling for calm, or expressing solidarity with allies. Discussions in bunkers protecting the planet's most important figures grew intense. Meanwhile, on the other side of the world, where the sun shone and light dissipated the dense ash cloud, broadcasts showed a dark space craft fixed blotch at the center of the sun —the Earth's heater.

Scientists around the globe offered guesses and theories. Some suggested solar magma detachments creating cosmic stars that collided with cities. Others declared the sun was cooling, sparking fears of an apocalypse. Believers prayed fervently, and the humblest among them claimed the blotch wasn't on the sun but closer —perhaps as near as the moon.

These latter were correct. While the sun moved, the blotch remained static, like a dirty glass on a table that no one moves. Some identified its oval shape, fueling speculation about UFOs and extraterrestrial attackers. Defense groups formed in every country, ready to face the unwelcome.

Skeptics, supported by religious groups dismissive of extraterrestrial theories, argued it was a prototype satellite weapon launched by one of the warring nations. This idea mobilized missiles aimed at space to shoot down the supposed war artifact. Amid the tension, presidents from affected and unaffected nations convened on secure communication lines to share reports. Pessimists predicted Earth's end; optimists hoped otherwise.

The U.S. president spoke decisively:

"We will prepare all weapons and attack when prudent, hoping the visitors descend from their ship to confront us with colonizing intentions. If they want this planet, let them come for it, but no one guarantees they will succeed alive."

Other leaders agreed. Armies prepared to defend Earth from an extraterrestrial attack. Broadcasts of the decision united citizens worldwide. Those trained for war became leaders, ready to protect the planet. Farmers and ranchers continued their work to sustain the war effort, while manufacturers produced weapons with unyielding determination. Human nature, inherently united, had been divided by habit; now, under this threat, it fought for its essence.

Homes braced for invaders. Cars lay abandoned, ships drifted, planes sat idle at airports, and guards watched vigilantly from buildings. Fear of another attack lingered. People remained on high alert, bullets chambered, ammunition belts like daily attire.

In the devastated cities, uncertainty reigned. Survivors had lost limbs; some crawled in search of help. Global aid campaigns struggled to reach everyone as panic consumed many. Volunteers arrived, determined to fight tragedy not with weapons but with compassion. They brought antibiotics, water, and limited food supplies.

Millions of corpses —men, women, children, and animals— littered the cities. Even rats hadn't escaped the massacre. Survivors among them turned cannibal, snouts smeared with blood and dust, their sharp teeth betraying deadly hunger. Dogs mimicked them, scavenging what they could. Some fought off rats to protect their dying owners.

The cities had become no man's land. Survival consumed everyone—humans, dogs, rats. While aid arrived, armed survivors defended themselves against cannibals, animals, and each other. Above it all, the looming threat hovered motionless beyond the sky, near the pale moon that illuminated the night.

Chapter IV

Twelve hours had passed since the violent attacks, and the world had plunged into mourning —some in silence, others with wailing cries akin to a mother lamenting a son sent to war who never returns or returns enclosed in a box draped with a flag, buried with honors as bullets pierce the air in a final salute.

It was then that the Knolots fell from the sky, like bolts from mythological gods. Clad in gleaming blue and silver armor, they made the ground tremble and buildings shift around them. Glass shattered thunderously, and the vibrations rippled as vividly as radiant blue neon in a dimly lit bar and silver that sparkled like stars piercing the darkness.

Citizens approached cautiously, taking cover behind cars and doors. Unarmed, some began to shoot. Bullets struck the Knolots fiercely, but the armored beings remained undisturbed, their suits impenetrable. Then, a citizen emerged armed with high-caliber weaponry, previously restricted for military use. Now, every human was a soldier, and no law forbade them from wielding such arms. He fired one thick bullet after another, but the Knolots stood motionless, just like the millions descending upon cities worldwide.

The military initiated tracking operations, employing GPS and cutting-edge technology. Missile-commanding generals observed the transmissions in disbelief. A general from Brazil launched a short-range missile at a Knolot, broadcasting the image for generals worldwide to witness. They watched as the missile vanished without explosion or explanation. The Knolot's blue beam had disintegrated every particle of iron and explosive material.

Panic gripped the onlookers. In underground bunkers, presidents, generals, and secretaries disconnected to confer in private. It was time to act decisively, to deploy the deadliest weapons. Missiles erupted from military encampments around the globe—short- and long-range projectiles soared into the sky.

The Knolots responded with precision. Small cannons emerged from their suits, shooting beams of blue light that disintegrated incoming missiles before they reached their targets. Armed citizens fired in desperation, hoping to distract the Knolots long enough for a missile to hit, but their efforts were met with scornful indifference.

As world leaders debated solutions in their bunkers, emotions ran high. Some wept openly; others begged for divine intervention. The cunning devised secondary plans—some to escape, others to surrender. The U.S. president established communication with Russian and Chinese leaders. They understood that their final move, though catastrophic, might be necessary. Facing impossible odds was the hallmark of heroes —those destined for eternal remembrance.

When plans solidified, the ship stationed before the sun opened its hatch. This time, only one figure emerged —a commander who possessed both eloquence and an understanding of other races. He descended like a dive bomber, accompanied by two dark clouds that moved at equal speed, plunging through Earth's atmosphere like Zeus's wrathful lightning. He landed directly on the White House, splitting it into rubble.

The dark clouds that accompanied him were not clouds at all but Medrian mist transports. Their occupants, cloaked in black robes and hoods, concealed their bodies entirely, revealing only dark gray skin like the void of space and hair resembling seaweed.

The Knolot commander strode through the wreckage of the White House and descended into the underground bunker.

The president's escort opened fire, but the bullets ricocheted harmlessly. The Knolot commander and the Medrians passed through every barrier effortlessly. In the bunker, the president stood tall, dressed in his tailored black suit adorned with the American flag pin, and demanded an explanation.

"Who are you, and why are you here? I demand an answer. You have mercilessly attacked the citizens of this planet with advanced weaponry, a cowardly act against defenseless people," the president declared.

The one in shining blue armor, marked by a silver star on his helmet, replied confidently: "Esteemed Mr. President of the United States, avail yourself of my presence to address your doubts, for my very presence alone should dispel them. If not, I would not be worthy to wear this armor —the most powerful of all— and those who now terrorize your planet would not call me commander."

"If you truly consider yourself a commander, you must understand the concept of honor," the president countered. "And if you do, you would know it is dishonorable to present yourself covered as you stand before one of this planet's leaders, even if you come to conquer."

"You are courageous, Mr. President. Very well, since you ask, I shall present myself."

The commander removed his helmet, revealing not a Knolot but a Medrian. His skin was the color of the universe, his hair like seaweed. His green eyes glowed faintly, and his nose, almost nonexistent, was nestled between high cheekbones and a thin mouth.

"My name is Ebrom. I am a resident of the planet Medrian, the same origin as King Perfidius of the Star. I command the army of Recruiters, selected from the three oldest planets: Medrian, Knolot, and Gelyant. Your planet had not yet spawned rational beings until recently."

His words resonated in the rest of the underground bunkers as communication remained open with other leaders, sparking doubts and confusion. Ebrom continued speaking, his tone measured yet faintly dismissive, as though the situation was beneath his notice.

"And since you have asked with authority, as a leader should, I will answer with the same authority. Among leaders, one can speak clearly.

"We have come here on the orders of King Perfidius, the possessor of the Eye of Amrok, to examine this planet. We had come before, but it was inhabited by irrational creatures that ate each other and fought incessantly with long teeth and dangerous hooves. That's why we attacked; we didn't know where to land. But now, discovering thinking beings, I deemed it necessary to descend and converse, for on all planets, words are valued, and explanations serve to reconcile nations and races.

"Among the decrees of King Perfidius, we have been ordered that if we find thinking beings, we should integrate them into our civilization, welcoming them into the system governed by His Majesty, allowing him to reign peacefully, as he does on other planets."

This is how Ebrom spoke, and the American president, like the others, listened in silence. Yet, in their minds, they sensed lies and deceit threaded through his words, like the empty promises of a merchant extolling only the virtues of his wares while hiding their defects. Thus, Ebrom, the Medrian leader of the Recruiters, sweetened their ears with carefully chosen words.

"And where is this king you speak of, and the system you mention?" asked the American president, his dark suit immaculate despite the chaos around him.

"King Perfidius is like no other creation of Amrok. He loves his subjects as himself, allowing them to live in peace, and the planets thrive with mutual assistance."

No one was convinced by the Medrian's saccharine words, but they knew they were powerless. Their weaponry had proven useless against these invaders.

"So, Mr. President and others present, as well as those listening from afar," Ebrom continued, "from today onward, King Perfidius will take control of this planet. As the commissioner on this mission, I will impose the rules that will govern, and all will seek happiness for all its habitants, for that is the sole purpose for which Amrok placed us here. There will be no opposition; we are prepared to suppress anyone harboring the intent to destroy a life filled with bliss."

Thus spoke Ebrom, and all fell silent, waiting for his final words, sensing they would be the most consequential. When he finished, he withdrew, followed by the Medrians in their dark cloud-like transports, retreating toward the ship from which they had descended.

In the ensuing days, peace reigned, but in the minds and hearts of humans, despair took root. Political and religious leaders, once telecommunications were restored, began addressing the population. The former, as was their custom, delivered speeches riddled with half-truths —some deceitful, others simply omitting the entire truth. Religious leaders framed the events as a divine test, anticipating the return of a savior who would free humanity from slavery, much like ancient times. Thus, everyone spoke, and the inhabitants moved with heads bowed and shoulders drooped, their spirits weighed down by resignation.

Each inhabitant formed long lines as instructed by the Recruiters, who subjected them to laser operations, implanting small trackers into their spines just below the brain. These immovable devices sent signals to the locators aboard the ship, capable of transmitting data anywhere in the universe—even to Knolot. From there, they monitored each individual's activity in real time.

Once the devices were in place, some inhabitants attempted to flee or resist the Recruiters. These incidents were swiftly suppressed, as any bearer of the tracker who defied the system was instantly disintegrated —exploding into a thousand pieces mid-air. Witnessing such horrors instilled terror in onlookers, who quickly understood that survival required compliance.

This persisted for six days as the Recruiters worked to cover the vast population. Those who resisted were hunted relentlessly using advanced reconnaissance techniques, like predators stalking prey. No one escaped. Humans hid beneath rocks, within caves, or in the ruins of their homes, but the Recruiters found them all and affixed trackers to every person they uncovered.

Chapter V

As soon as the ominous mood enveloped the minds of everyone gathered around Axel —the young man with blue lines on his legs— a gust of vivid memories swept through the restaurant, famous for its fresh donuts and daily coffee. Thousands of ghosts surrounded the living, attempting to communicate that they were now better, no longer trapped in an invented reality and invisible to the human eye. They lingered there, doing what ghosts do: imitating the living without purpose.

Ammy couldn't take her eyes off the television. She pulled her state-of-the-art white mobile phone from her purse. When she raised it to her face to identify the numbers, she noticed liquid drops falling onto the screen. These drops sprouted from her face, like a watering can showering rose bushes before sunrise. It was then, with the help of the phone's reflection, that she realized she was crying fervently. She hated reporting deaths.

Ammy glanced at the impassive face of the young man who had just appeared. He stared expressionlessly into her eyes, like a fledgling looking at its mother before being tossed out of the nest for the first time, waiting for an explanation of how to move its wings. She understood immediately.

Reaching into her wallet, she took out a twenty-dollar bill and left it on the table. Then she asked her guest to stand, which he did hastily. However, Ammy squeezed his hand and forced him to walk slowly, knowing that everyone was suspicious and prone to either run for shelter or flee the country.

"What's happening?" asked the distressed reporter outside the restaurant, from which a smell of burnt bread emanated.

"The recruiters' army has arrived," the young man replied. "My father had mentioned it, but I remained incredulous because I hadn't witnessed their existence. Now I know, and I believe his words. Participating in those not-so-distant wars of this time has served him well.

"Now, listen to my words, Miss Amanda Ríos. Soon, life as you know it on this planet will change. Societies will collapse. Beliefs will cease to exist —or there will be conflict among them— and new ones will emerge. All of this will happen in less than seven earthly days, because on other planets, time is not measured. It arrives and never leaves."

So spoke the young man who had disappeared fourteen years before, prophesying an end and a new beginning. His words only confused the respected blogger further as she held her phone, debating whether to call her editor or check on her friends to inquire about their well-being.

"What do you mean by this, Axel? Your words are unclear, lack meaning, and you haven't convinced me of your stay while you were missing, nor the purpose of your return. So, please, I beg you to be more concise in your expressions. A good shepherd is better understood than a good politician, although both speak of laws and in their speeches exist lies or words that disguise the truth."

That's how Miss Ríos expressed herself, as she was known to the younger ones who worked for her and others she encountered on the street or in a local bookstore.

"Please, forgive the confusion I've caused you, as I haven't engaged in conversation with humans before, except for my father minutes before our return to planet Earth. However, I will explain in more detail, as you've requested.

"According to my father, it is time for the Eye of Amrok, creator of universes, to choose a new King. For this reason, the current king, Perfidius, originating from Medrian, the first planet of this infinite universe, has decided to recruit all the candidates —eight in total, as there are two from each planet.

"He has also implanted the idea of monitoring the movements of all beings inhabiting each of the planets. When the Eye of Amrok chooses where to fall, he can retrieve it, as he is eager for power and intends to live forever, as those who sit with Amrok do, residing where there is no time, and space is infinite."

This was the response of the orphaned son at birth, anticipating the blogger's next question, continuing the explanation.

"My father, who sacrifices everything for ideals and is foolish in keeping alive the utopian concepts of freedom founded in this place and for which he fought in recent wars —dressed as a soldier, according to his own account— has brought me to this place, Earth, in search of refuge. Neither Knolots nor Medrians could live here; for they feed on a different light, less warm than the one the sun radiates, covering us from head to toe and sustaining life. Besides, they feed on other things nonexistent on the terrestrial globe, unknown even to chemists and alchemists.

"They don't breathe oxygen, don't drink water but crystals or darkened mud, and their blood is not red like ours, for they are akin to the universe and distant from mammals. So this, those who rebel against the terrible power of Perfidius thought, would be a perfect refuge to await the star's fall on any planet it chooses. For it is the Creator's eye, and he sees everything."

Thus spoke John Flames' son and fell silent, feeling the others very close to them, filling the coffee. They watched the flickering images reflected on the TVs, dialing numbers repeatedly with mobile phones in hand, desperate. Many didn't get answers, and those who managed to communicate cried, besieged by the joy of finding someone on the other end of the phone. But various feelings invaded them, finding and colliding with each other, as it's not easy to see someone cry for a loss and be happy because you find your own.

Meanwhile, many took to the streets, losing their space, which was taken by another pair of feet eager for news. The hallway was wetter than when it rains in October or freezes the streets in the month of February, and tear drops kept falling, melting any good humor coming from hope.

The reporter signaled to Axel that they should leave the place, and he complied without resistance, not even uttering a word, for words choked in his throat. Still unaware of why, he felt an internal connection with those unhappy souls who were bitterly sobbing. She held his left hand, intertwining their fingers over the wrist, and they walked silently behind her until they crossed the crystalline threshold, fogged by sweat and cleansed with saline substance from the floors.

Both walked along the sidewalk until they reached a phone booth, which was swaying, as dozens of people urged the speaker to end their call, waving from inside while others moved it with hands and feet. It was chaotic outside, as everyone was afraid, fearing to be the next extinct city.

They sat on a bench, which unsurprisingly was empty, for who has time to sit in a crisis of such magnitude? Perhaps some politician, preparing a rescue plan, but they were far from there. So, when they found themselves alone, the blogger looked into the young man's restless hair and eyes, waiting for him to continue his story, and so he did.

"However, they were wrong, as the Knolot ships, which are capable of coming and going, are also capable of staying. And the recruiter's suits are resistant to everything; therefore, there is no place to hide. Now I understand it, and I believe everyone does the same; there is no refuge far enough from Perfidius' eyes.

"Still, it is necessary to try, my father told me so, and he was told by those who remain in the fight on the other side of the planet Knolot, where not even hope is standing, and they have to live on what remains, and the only refuge is the abandoned train station."

"What do you mean by trying? Tell me, your words are confusing, especially in these chaotic times. If your decision is to fight, then wait until they call you, along with everyone else, to war, for it's clear that after this there will be war, and unlike your predictions, I predict something worse, as the responsible one will fall; whether from this world or another, they will not go unpunished. Then you can fight, like those you speak of.

"But if you intend to flee and hide, then you are not in the right place; this country is built with heroes, and those like your father who fought and fought to maintain freedom will rise again and prevail, in our side is the only God, whom we worship, and there is no other beside Him, and the only ones who sit by His side are those who fall and die in His name."

This was Amanda Ríos's patriotic response.

"So much inconsistency in your words, Miss Ríos, but it is not my task to contradict you, for I am here with a purpose, one that you judge dishonorable, and I will fulfill it only with your help. For everything around me is unknown, and one cannot go blindly without first asking for their destination.

"It is my understanding that not far from here, inhabitants of the planet Gelyant dwell, those with dense hair and sharp claws; and it is my intention to reach them, as they will provide us shelter. If it is in your spirit to accompany me, otherwise, the only favor I require is to guide me to that point, and then you embark on whatever direction your reason dictates."

"If this is all you require of me, I will gladly guide you and accompany you to the limits of the place you undoubtedly intend to reach. But do not ask me to take refuge in such a place, for my spirit forbids it, and my purpose is what guides my profession.

"So, once you reach your destination, I will continue my path and inform everyone about what is happening, delivering truthful news—something sorely lacking in today's media. Information that reflects the truth, not embellished scenarios and well-orchestrated theaters to keep information consumers growing in ignorance. So, reveal to me the place you intend to go, and I will stand guard until you arrive."

Ammy spoke with courage in her words, and it was not simulated courage. She had demonstrated bravery covering war and terrorism notes in places where anarchy and worse reigned. As soon as she finished her sentence, Axel, the orphaned son, named Allegheny National Forest as his destination. Surprised, the blogger took her phone and, using the navigation system, located the place and directions on how to get there.

Under normal conditions, the journey would take a maximum of eight hours, taking traffic into account. However, these were not normal conditions, and analyzing what was already evident, it would take at least half a day, if not a bit more, to arrive. Nevertheless, she took it lightly, as she did not expect it to be so close, and they both walked toward where her car was parked.

• • •

John, as soon as he left the reporter's apartment—who had followed his case for over a decade and was now handing over his son to guide him to his destination—shed the last tears he would shed in his life. He was separating again from the only connection he had left with his wife who died in childbirth, but he couldn't stay. The Recruiters, the army in service to King Perfidius, were still tracking him and pursuing him closely.

Under the stairs that had served him to climb, as he did not expect the Recruiters, in blue and silver suits, to use that means to reach him (as they had abilities superior to walking or standing, defying gravity and the physical laws governing this planet), he emerged on the outskirts of the apartment complex, surrounded by an innumerable crowd. He did not hesitate to seize a mobile phone, snatching it without warning from a pedestrian who continued on his way, having been violated, for fighting was not in his nature but the opposite.

John remembered the time before his disappearance when he acquired a mobile phone of larger proportions than the one he held now. He needed to stay in touch with his pregnant wife. As a mercantile marine defending his homeland, he was always far away, absent. He then dialed the only phone number he remembered, stamped on his left forearm, marked with his own hand and a deliberately borrowed knife, understanding that he would need it when those beings with snowy skin, inhabitants of the planet Knolot, implanted the tracker in his spine and expressed the impossibility of removing it. Since then, he knew.

The phone rang three times as John walked hurriedly, pressed against the dark alley wall. By the fourth ring's turn, a raspy and light voice answered on the other end, and without waiting for a response, John interrupted.

"James. Listen to me now after so long, for time is what I have the least and what I lack the most right now. I am John," spoke the widowed father, and on the other end, James listened attentively, his former marine squadron companion. When they served together in wars not too distant in Earth's timeline and retired from military affairs, one became a surgeon while the other fervently fell in love with his son's mother.

"I will speak to you honestly because my word is all I have left. My wife died in childbirth, and today, by my own will and for purposes beyond any explanation I can give you, I have placed the fate of the child, mine and hers, in other hands. So, listen to me to the end. If you find doubt in my words, remember how many times we doubted our own testimonies during the war, yet despite that, I had your back, and you did the same for me.

"That's why I call you. If we ever owed each other or were brothers in battle, don't hang up the phone, for what I'm about to tell you is, by itself, incredible. But, as I tell you, I hope you make an exception and open your mind to things that cannot be proven."

In a hurry with his words, John spoke as he walked through dark alleys, always fleeing. The other side awaited an explanation, even though he feared, with a cold sweat on his forehead, knowing this explanation, as other former comrades had contacted him days before. Nevertheless, he remained prudent because he understood manners and perceived the precipitated behavior with which John spoke.

"I need a safe place, but by this, I mean isolated, not protected, like the camps on the battlefield. I'm talking about a place where no electronic signal can enter or leave; be it voice or data and electricity, because they are after me. And I also need your surgeon's hands because I trust you with my life, like someone who walks forward in war, confident that no one will attack from behind because someone guards that flank. I stay focused on my task; that's how much confidence I have in you.

"In my spine, there's an electronic device embedded that transmits my location. So, the operation must be quick, and about the pain, don't rush because I understand what someone goes through when their skin is opened, and organs are violated by hands other than their own, to obtain objects that don't belong to them. In other instances, I had various bullets made of led, so hot they burned everything around them.

"Thus, now that you've heard, respond to my pleas and accept everything I say as the truth. I wouldn't poison my tongue with auditory venom, even if I were captured by rebel troops and tortured day and night to obtain a confession from my lips. As you know, we're both trained to provide only our credentials."

"John, my friend, what you're saying is no surprise to me. Arthur contacted me hours ago and scheduled a meeting for today. If you had called three minutes later, you wouldn't have found me. In a secure place, impenetrable even to data transmissions, he hasn't explained the reason for the insistence, but he said it's a matter of life or death. He has gathered a small group of former comrades, asked about you, but I had no answer as I didn't know your whereabouts. But let's talk no more. Give me your location, and there will be time for detailed explanations once we meet in the bunker."

John Flames explained how to reach him after seeing the directions on the top of the posts at the corners. Since he shouldn't stay still, they agreed to meet three miles from that place.

So the pursued, John, spent half an hour hiding among cars, zigzagging through buildings, alleys, and roads, until finally, a familiar blue van with tinted windows intercepted him. His former companion signaled for him to climb in.

Once on board, they skipped greetings. James moved to the back seat and kindly asked his wife not to look back. This side of the car was about to be stained with dark blood. He also recommended her to ignoring the screams, as it wouldn't be a painless operation, quite the opposite. He handed a bottle of aged Scottish whiskey to the former marine, who, as a fugitive, fled and sought to break free from the chains that tied him to that endless pursuit.

Then, from his briefcase, he took out a portable ultrasound machine, which resembled a "flip-flop" mobile phone, and began to scan the entire back until, deep within all the tissues, veins, and muscles, he identified the tracker. He saw it extremely small, as small as a larva, but this larva, the former military surgeon imagined, had the utility of a complete machine.

He envisioned a computer reduced to a fraction of its size, with programmers sitting in front of it entering commands through the keyboard, instructing it to keep moving, and then sending the signal to a master server so that they and the information never got lost.

Then he interrupted the reverie and, with an unwavering pulse, inserted the scalpel just above the tracker and quickly pierced it. Pain takes time to reach the brain, and he wanted to take advantage of the time it took for it to travel through all the nerves and loop around the body to retrieve it. When he reached it, he couldn't remove it because it was tightly attached to the Axis, as if it were glued with "super glue" or worse, screwed into this cervical bone.

The pain then reached John's brain, and he started screaming as if he were being killed or having his nails pulled out with square-tipped tweezers slowly. Blood, naturally, sprayed all over his back, covering his hands, which were, in turn, covered with blue latex gloves.

The woman at the wheel, upon hearing the screams, tried to turn around, but when she saw the dark red blood on her husband's hands and face, she focused on the steering wheel. She would have to drive for at least an hour through curves and slopes, so she didn't turn around anymore.

The surgeon asked his friend to drink from the bottle, as it would help relax the nerves, as sweet whiskey is not only a party booster but also the host of sleep. John obeyed because the desire to stop being pursued was stronger than the pain of feeling death nearby, for when you are chased and struggle to hide, the best hiding place after trying everything is non-existence. However, that was far from happening.

James took more tools from his briefcase, and with the help of separators, wire scissors, and forceps, he managed to extract it. Then he threw it out of one of the windows and quickly began to heal the wound, like vultures that immediately, after the predator finishes feeding, surrender to the corpse to claim the remains. His hands were agile, and soon he was suturing it with special thread. When finished, they looked into each other's eyes, the trust of old friends evident. John handed the bottle to James' left hand, and they clasped both right hands.

"Pleasure to see you," they said, and the widowed father reclined while the ex-military surgeon did the same as they awaited their destination. The woman at the wheel meticulously searched for the given address, like a lioness stalking a gazelle, patiently examining each of the numbers on the back of the houses, fearing any mistake or confusion among the neighbors.

Suddenly, all the residents came out of their houses, the road resonated with the voices in unison from the televisions, but this was obstructed by the wind and impossible for James' wife to hear clearly. The other two, still with high levels of adrenaline, tried to calm their pulses, and the surgeon checked the vital signs of the freshly operated.

Some cars began moving on the same road she was traveling, and like ants following each other, they went above the trail of smoke and the smell of burnt fuel left by the first. The family van was engulfed by a crowd of cars in a hurry, bombarding it with arrogant honking sounds, distracting her because if it's difficult to be lost, it's even harder to be under stress.

Finally, when she found the house with the correct number, she drove the vehicle as close to the door as possible, not intending to cause more panic than she already sensed on the roads if people saw her husband and the friend she carried in the back seat, both covered in blood. The door of the house opened as they got out, and between James and his wife, they lowered John's almost lifeless body.

Upon entering, John opened his eyes, greeted Arthur, and he received him with joy, as if he had been expecting him. The house was only a facade because they immediately headed for the door leading to the basement. They descended the stairs slowly. The light was intermittent, as panic ruled the entire city, and emergency generators were just beginning to work. At that moment, they only knew that several cities had been attacked with weapons of mass destruction.

Arriving in the underground room, John observed that Arthur had built a small room right in the middle of the foundation and the first floor. It could accommodate fewer than ten people and was covered outside with a shiny material, similar to when you wrap a good piece of lamb before putting it in the oven with aluminum foil. All four walls shone; even the tile below the first floor could be seen, and it, too, glowed.

Everyone covered their eyes at the same time, even John, who kept them closed most of the time due to the combination of pain, the cell recovery process trying to heal the wounds, and the alcohol he had used to boost his courage and endurance. From the inside emerged a huge figure, at least five feet taller than the tallest present, presumably James, the surgeon who held his wounded friend by the shoulder. This giant was covered with silver armor with ornaments that seemed alive, changing position as it advanced toward them and shining in golden tones.

From the armor emanated a light akin to the sun, illuminating the room and reflecting on the shiny surface. Nanorobots, small as metallic pellets, detached from the armor and clustered in the hands, creating metallic gloves that shone like gold and silver jewelry. The armor dissolved entirely, revealing the snow-white skin of the face, which all inhabitants of the planet Knolot bear from birth to death. Everything, except a respirator covering the nose and mouth, connecting to a metal tube leading to a small tank at the waist, containing the gases on which their lives depended.

"You've done it!" he spoke enthusiastically with a soft, pleasant voice. He approached John, and though weak, adrenaline boosting his spirits, John lifted his face to see him. When face to face, he recognized him: that giant was none other than a Knolot. He smiled broadly, as if he had found a companion on the battlefield still alive. The Knolot placed his hand on the back of the wounded human, and hundreds of nanorobots moved around, starting to saturate the wound from the inside, connecting every ligament and fiber of the body.

"Anyway, you need to rest," said the extraterrestrial, not native to this planet but from an older one. He lifted John as if he were made of paper, relieving James and his wife of the weight, both sweating profusely. He settled him on one of the bunk beds they had installed beforehand. Feeling the mattress, John surrendered to sleep and slumbered peacefully, like children who, after a bad dream, go to their parents' bed feeling safe and protected. The widowed father slept for six uninterrupted hours, while the others caught up on the news and devised the plan against the recruiters and King Perfidius.

Chapter VI

When Axel and the reporter reached the car, she gestured for him to get in, completely forgetting the origin of the dark-skinned youth. It's common for civilized people, and sometimes in wild animals, to assume that others they interact with are similar in intellect and experience. Like a lion attacking another, assuming that the other will attack first, Amanda Ríos expected that by simply indicating him to get into the car, he would open the door, sit in the passenger seat, and fasten his seatbelt.

However, it was an unpleasant surprise to hear the roof of the car sink when Axel's heavy feet landed on it. Startled by the sharp sound of the metal contracting and the thud of the feet, she thought they might have been attacked, and an explosive had fallen nearby. She threw herself to the ground, only to get up seconds later with a flushed face, like the interior of a ripe watermelon. Amid hysterical complaints, she demanded Axel descend carefully, fearing the windshield might shatter. Axel obeyed and carefully went down of the vehicle.

The reporter, still scared and with trembling hands, went to the other end of the car to open the door and instruct him on how to get in and take a seat. After closing the door, as she walked to the driver's side, she reflected on what had happened. She concluded that it wasn't the young man's fault since you can't blame someone who is unaware; however, this logic only applies to moral issues, not legal ones.

Ammy got into the car, started it, and tuned in to the first station on the radio to stay informed about what was happening around her. She adjusted the volume and began to drive with her silent copilot sitting upright at ninety degrees, his legs illuminated by the blue glow of the lines that facilitated his walking.

The sun, that hot and beautiful star, bearer of the vital warmth of the Milky Way, a giant ball of fire visible from the remotest places, like the dawn illuminating this part of the planet, rose like plants from a buried seed. Meanwhile, Axel continued to look around, like a child in front of the variety of colors in a bakery, imagining each flavor in his mouth.

Amanda, relaxing her legs and listening to the news, found no signs of the army on the state highway. Perhaps they had focused primarily within the cities, monitoring the entrances and exits to detect the enemy before being attacked. However, Axel remained pensive, observing his surroundings, eager to get out and run to discover what that place was made of, like a child looking at candies but unable to taste them.

"Why, when the café's television broadcasted the attacks of the Recruiter army, did the people gathered there? Is it because one of their body parts was hurting? For I have shed the hot drops from my eyes when I was a child, influenced by the punishment of one of the Knolots who kindly took care of me. However, that time I disobeyed their orders, and they inflicted great pain on me through an almost invisible ray, torturing the skin that covers my entrails.

"But those around us cried with greater sorrow, barely noticeable, as it tends to store in the soul, as it is known in this world, the electric spark that keeps the body alive. Is it possible that pain can be inflicted at great distances? Or is there an external force punishing their body while others, warlike, attack and exterminate entire cities?" So spoke the young man with bronze skin and tousled hair, breaking the silence that had accompanied them throughout the journey.

This question disoriented the driver, who kept her eyes on the road while listening to the hum of helicopters approaching the exit of the federal highway. They were approaching exit 111, and she didn't steer the conversation away. She remained silent as she turned the steering wheel, and the car glided along the US-219. When the map on her mobile phone indicated they should go straight, she slowed down and looked into the eyes of that naive young man.

"You are naive about human behaviors since you've been separated from them since birth. Poor you, not suffering from the tragedy of others, condemned to lack feelings. Axel, for years, people have tried to explain the difference between the soul and the body; however, this mystery lacks validity because there is no separation. And if there were, then we would be condemned to cruelty, and thought would be separated from reason. These two would completely eliminate one feelings.

"But you, an innocent children unaware of the customs and history of this planet, lacking earthly memories, where wars and destruction were glorified not long ago, and for the sake of these trivialities, millions of people died at the hands of cruel murderers. Now, the memory is bring back to life and hurts the inhabitants of the world from within, for although it is distant in time, it is not far in our memory. And worried about their loved ones in the cities, they fear for their well-being. That's why anguish invades them to the point of tears." Answered the reporter, still driving on the empty main road without any trace of living beings. "It's strange, there are no people fleeing this place," she vaguely said.

"Incoherent to me is what you've said because anguish, like sensation and memory, is insubstantial. These are only part of something insensitive that affects the body and the mind only when hungry or when one of the body's natural needs is not met. And you speak of history and customs, and due to the lack of these, you have excluded me from the race to which I supposedly belong. I consider, then, that you must be right in your thoughts because I have not grown up among humans.

"Although my anatomy is identical to theirs, I cannot belong to them if I lack such social concepts as you refer to. So tell me what I am, for, like a human and any mammal, I sit in your car, but I differ from Medrians, the first inhabitants of the universe, and Knolots of snowy skin, experts in sciences, and the Gelyants, of whom I've only been fortunate to see one, for he was locked in a glass cube next to mine. They have, by their own description, for he spoke to me that time they moved him to another place, a great heart and only think of peace. They are covered in hair, and their eyes are brown, just like their skin."

"No, Axel, don't doubt your lineage, for you are the son of humans and, therefore, human to the core. But it is necessary to teach you what this means, and although little time remains for us, there will be time for you to learn. When you finally understand how your feelings connect with your thoughts and the heart, which in your reasoning is nothing more than a vital organ, can also make decisions. And when these decisions are based on what your heart feels, the world becomes a better place, and reason is dominated by beauty.

"Then, you, John Flames' son, will become a complete human. As such, you will defend this Earth and stand in front of anyone, just to give them the opportunity to decide whether they want to kneel before such a tyrant, capable of destroying entire cities, or fight against such evil."

So spoke Amanda Ríos, trying to dispel all misconceptions and pessimistic ideas, injecting courage into his mind. She turned the steering wheel from side to side, avoiding cars parked in the middle of the road, and finally saw signs of life in the houses. Although these did not manifest corporeally, behind the windows, barricaded and covered with firm and thick wooden boards, you could see the eyes of some, as if they were surveillance cameras in a convenience store moving from side to side, depending on where the customer is.

All to have a better view of what he is doing; that's how those eyes watched them. But only sporadically, as the noise of the helicopter blades frightened their minds, and they recoiled from the windows, fearing some attack or reprisal from the government due to the martial law in effect.

The last turn she made was to the left on Highway 79, and a few meters ahead, the entrance to the immense Allegheny National Forest. The forest unfolded, majestic and imposing, brimming with trees.

"Here is where you asked me to take you, and so I have; however, this is also where I must leave you. Other matters claim my attention, as my profession demands. I have to follow the news, seek answers. Although I know I will find some with you, I'm not sure if they are the most suitable. It's not the same to get information from a soldier as from a general. The latter has more experience, backing, and the trust of their superiors. Moreover, they handle classified and specific information. Therefore, I need to go back and locate my team of communicators to find answers."

This is how Ammy expressed herself, and Axel listened, understanding every word and thought. He understood that not even she knew why she returned to Earth. Axel shook her hand, imitating the gesture of those who greeted each other in the café. No one, even if proud to belong to a society, is exempt from imitation; on the contrary, it's as natural as breathing. He thanked her sincerely, and his eyes reflected that.

Then, Axel headed into the forest, and Amanda Ríos returned to the car, driving back on roads filled with cars and sparse in living beings, with eyes watching from windows covered with crossed timbers.

Chapter VII

Axel still found himself immersed in confusion as he ventured into the vast forest, akin to one who discovers deception but debates within whether to believe it or not. It's the kind of turmoil that arises when trust is given and fears of losing it linger. Thoughts of non-belonging assailed Axel, akin to a fish already carried away by the current or ensnared in delicate silken nets, out of water, struggling to breathe but finding it impossible.

His respiratory system wouldn't allow it, moving inconsistently, wavering between life and death. The newcomer to Earth experienced something similar, unaccustomed to open spaces, feeling suffocated amid thoughts of growth, reminiscing about the white Knolots that fed him behind extended layers of glass.

Yet, what tormented him the most was not that, but the lack of identity. Something worse than loneliness, generating a void that sank and dragged, like in quicksand, losing itself in the darkness of emptiness and ending up mimicking others, be they animals or plants. A flavorless life, where one doesn't live but merely survives.

The young orphaned youth was on the verge of being absorbed by that black hole, if not for the long arms that emerged from the pine's crown against which he leaned. With thick, sharp claws, they gripped his ribs and, in a single thrust, propelled him into the azure sky. Surprised, Axel let out a desperate scream, frightening the pigeons clinging to the branches.

For a moment, he closed his eyes, but upon realizing he hadn't jumped willingly, he tried to grab onto a branch during his fall. He failed, hitting his arms and hands. Then, the long-armed being that propelled him positioned itself beside him, embraced him around the waist, and guided him from tree to tree. Axel, attempting to strike or push the being away, failed and opted for using words, hoping it would understand.

He observed the light brown eyes, the same color as the polished center of a tree. He felt the hairs on the bare, sun-kissed arms, vast and golden.

"You must let me go. I'm not here looking for trouble. I prefer to talk on solid ground, not at these heights. The wind belongs to the birds and beings that, with their minds, can move objects like the Knolots. They are not governed by gravitational laws; they can break and modify them at will."

"Don't worry, Axel. We are the ones you've come to find, and we were expecting you. It was time for you to appear; we were beginning to doubt the wisdom of our group's prudent leader, the venerable Lido, tutor to the natural candidate of the Eye of Amrok on the planet Gelyant. As interpreted from King Kendorf's orders, conveyed verbally to his brother but ingrained in each of the candidates. We await the selection of the new guardian, the upcoming queen who will possess the star, and then the order of the universe will be restored."

So spoke the gallant warrior Debki from the planet Gelyant, leading him to a hidden cave amidst trees and rocks. He recalled his father's orders as he followed her inside, observing her hunched back, her way of walking, and the peculiarity of her appearance.

"It is both a pleasure and a misfortune to meet you, Axel Flames. The cruelty that robs a human of the precious gift of childhood is as vast as it is unfathomable. Those who live fast regret not being able to turn back, for imagination fills the voids that societal questions in this world fail to cover. They settle for sustenance, not even thinking about it while they have fun or play. It's only when the body demands it that they reach out.

But you, unfortunate one, lost your mother and the paternal love your father was willing to give you was snatched away. They traded it for glass walls, raised you like a pet, teaching you tricks like parakeets to repeat senseless words. Thus they made you, oh unfortunate one. The culprit of such atrocity is ambition, clouding the mind of the most prudent once they taste power firsthand. That was done by the one who now reigns in the universe, more powerful than Kendorf, for his intentions are malign, and his army is endless.

And you, unfeeling one, lack the human heart because you did not grow up in a place belonging to this civilization. You are exempt from the characteristic feelings of the race that populates and rules this planet, even though it does so blindly and irrationally. Still, goodness surpasses the limits of ambition. Within each of them, despite ethical and moral struggles, coherence always prevails.

You, unhappy one, have missed this, and your brain has been filled with ice and equally cold ideas, incapable of demonstrating love, as the Knolots base their ideals on machines, which they cherish more than their own planet. Oh, exploring child, you have suffered so much, and the worst in your destiny is yet to come.

Not only did you lose your mother and lack identity, but you will also fight alongside those who believe in good and the restoration of order. But doubt will always linger in your mind and heart about whether this is right, and you will be tempted to step back. We all have doubts, and when they arise, they make us think and fear reason.

Because doubt is stronger in essence, slandering truth and sympathizing with internal fears, those that, despite being unknown, hide in the tangles of the brain and paralyze the muscles when they decide to emerge, block ideas, and do not allow the body to function. But come closer, let my eyes see you more clearly, for beneath these rocks, light is scarce, and my vision, over time, has weakened, as nothing in the universe is infinite. It was created by an Eternal, and what they create tends to be destroyed, either by time or the hands of vile beings like Perfidius, oh thieving King."

Axel, fearful, walked toward the elderly Gelyant who extended his right hand to greet him properly. The cave's light came from deeper within and the gaps that allowed the radiant sun to pass through. Moreover, occasionally, from the inside of the young man's coat, the blue light of the lines that kept his legs straight escaped, changing color. The teeth and eyes of everyone gleamed.

He noticed that it wasn't just him, Debki, and Lido, but also a younger Gelyant than all and a sturdy Gelyant, short in stature but with great muscles. When he stood in front of the elder, he noticed that both the face and skull were covered in endless and long strips of hair, thinner than a pin but well-populated and the same color as the eyes. Unlike Debki, he had short arms and lacked claws on his hands.

"Tell me, elder, what is your name and why do you know of my existence? Has my father come to see you before me and fled from the Recruiters who pursue him through the tracker? Or do you possess divine foresight, characteristic of Gelyants, like moving objects with the mind and through chips embedded in their napes, like the Knolots?"

"Oh chosen one of Amrok's eye! It was not your father who brought the news of your arrival, nor do I possess what you refer to as divine, the gift of foresight. This is reserved for the one who holds the star and can only use it if Amrok, the creator, allows it, for he sees everything, even when not present.

But as you ask what your mind dictates and this is the first doubt that springs to your lips, I will answer it to delay the meals no further, for after we all satisfy our hunger and thirst, we must leave this place. It is necessary, for those who watch everything from beyond the sky already know our refuge, and if it weren't for Debki who protects us, they would have attacked us by now.

Now, with the presence of Ebrom, who is more powerful as he comes from Medrian and is protected by a Knolot suit, they will have no reason to stop their attack.

It is necessary that I tell you that the former King, Larks, is on this planet, exiled by Perfidius when he seized the Eye of Amrok with the help of the Knolot Scepter. Larks found a way to communicate with the rebels of that planet where they kept you captive, not only you but also the other candidate born in Turkey, a place you are unfamiliar with since you have just arrived. He was also abducted at birth, and his mother died in childbirth.

Those who rebel against Perfidius and wisely protected the candidates from that planet, training them to be king, as we prepared Agui." Lido paused and pointed with his narrowed eyes to his left, where the young Gelyant was located, who did not take her eyes off the floor, fearing to disrespect the tenant or her oldest tutor.

"It was they who notified him of your existence and your escape. He, in turn, contacted Debki, and through her, he informed us of your arrival and your instructions to find us. You have arrived at an unfortunate time because now that they attack us, you will have to flee and search again. Agui will go with you, and if it weren't for Debki, who is a warrior and the only one with the strength and skill to defend us since on our planet, women are stronger and more skilled in war, and men sow and harvest the fields, she would go with you.

But please, go ahead and eat and satisfy your hunger, for it will be a long journey ahead."

So spoke the senile Gelyant, directing them further in, where there was a white fire that surprisingly emitted no heat, only pure light.

There was Yana, Lido's wife, preparing food. She had long arms and sharp claws, and her hair cascaded down to her ankles. She hurried them to serve food and then handed a backpack to Agui, which she placed on her back.

First, the earth trembled, followed by a deafening noise inside and outside the cave. Stones began to move, and rocks of all sizes fell from above in all directions, like raindrops falling from the sky. Sand and rocks fell incessantly, leaving no space untouched. Lido's legs also trembled, as did the spirits of all present, except for Debki and Axel.

The warrior enjoyed when danger loomed, as she was trained for it, and one who knows no fear is never afraid. Their bodies do not react like the brave or the coward, for fear, though a contradiction, is a natural sensation in every living being, either by instinct or habit.

Leading everyone to the rear exit, the elder moved like a turtle without hurry, or if he had any, his muscles did not respond, for he was slow of pace. Debki lifted him with her long arms and also took Yana, who was at the end of the line, behind Jormer with sturdy arms. Agui leaped, using claws on feet and hands to propel his body, leading the way with his mother.

Axel, who didn't understand the urgency, as his nervous system did not warn him of danger, followed closely using the enhancers attached to the skin of his legs. These helped him make long jumps, and with his arms, he made his way while avoiding the rocks that fell, one after another or all together, as they obey no law but gravity that only attracts bodies from above downward.

When they finally exited the cave, the splendor of the sun illuminated their faces, and the Gelyants shone as if made of bronze, the color of their hair reflected the light. Debki climbed the tallest tree using only her feet, for both arms were occupied. Agui waited for Jormer to arrive and took him by the waist with his left arm. He took him to the top of the tree while Axel watched, leaping from one tree to another, aided by his enhancers. Leveling his body with his hands, he reached the same place where the Gelyant warrior left the elders, and Agui carried Jormer.

"It is advisable that you leave now; Agui has instructions on how to find King Larks, who is guarded by the guardian of the sea. Someone was recently sent by Perfidius to capture him and not allow him to intervene in the selection of the new possessor of the Eye of Amrok. However, you must reach him, and when you do, he will show you the way to the powerful eye of the Creator.

As the best guide who teaches his apprentices to survive, she will guide you to victory, and finally, harmony will reign in all these planets united by the same creator and separated only by distance and evil"

So spoke Lido with a raspy and trembling voice, still shaken by the impression of being swallowed by that collapsing cave.

Debki, whose blood boiled and her heart beat strongly, hugged her daughter, saying goodbye as only mothers say goodbye to their offspring when they understand the danger and the slim chance of seeing them again. She embraced her, embedding her claws slightly, applying much force as if wanting to merge in skin and breath. She spoke tenderly:

"Oh, my daughter! Chosen by the Creator to follow in the footsteps of King Kendorf, let this hug be a show of my love for you, and if it were the last, remember me as I remember your father.

Dead in our escape at the hands of he who craves eternal life and dares to compare himself to Amrok, or those who live beside him outside of this universe and amid others. May I, as long as I live, fight for you to have a choice and, with a sensible heart, act as a queen —the best who has ruled the universe."

Thus she spoke, and thick, warm tears fell from her eyes as well as those of her daughter, and in seconds, the five Gelyants who sought refuge there, awaiting the army of Recruiters, joined in tears.

Agui uttered no words, for when hugged with enough force and there is love in the gaze, that is enough to convey in silence all that can be omitted with words. And they all understood, everyone except Axel, who watched motionless from the treetop.

The warlike impulse seized Debki, and she left the group to hasten the encounter with the Recruiters who were closely pursuing them. It was a logical strategy, for the farther from Agui and Axel, the more likely they were to escape. She positioned herself in front of them, forcing them to turn their backs to those who would attempt to flee.

However, Axel, more by instinct than by desire or a sense of concern, as he lacked these as well, followed her jumps. As soon as she stopped, he did too, at her side. Right above them was Ebrom, and two others were destroying the forest with blue and red rays, and trees fell at their feet.

Just like those who lose in a battle and, seeking mercy, bow at the feet of the victor begging for their lives, and the victors decide if they live or die, for they have the power and strength that victory bestows —thus, the trees piled at their feet, for they had lost a battle fought for hundreds of years, in which they had fought to stay standing. But the Recruiters are more powerful than any other attack wrought by nature or the law of man's protection.

Meanwhile, Agui caught up with them and pulled the trench coat covering Axel's body from behind. Placing his index finger on his lips, he indicated that he should remain silent. This fight did not concern them; their duty was to flee and try to win the war. For although retreat is never honorable, sometimes it is necessary, especially if the plan warrants it, and greater impact results are expected.

Debki glanced at them, and seeing that her daughter had everything under control, she did not hesitate to attack one of the Recruiters who, on foot, was destroying the forest. Just like a lioness hunting its prey —a deer watching it for endless hours under the relentless sun and covering itself with dry grass that camouflages its fur; just when it notices a moment of weakness in the deer that prevents it from running faster than the feline's muscles— it attacks, always with its jaws focused on the neck and claws sunk into the chest or jugular, putting all its weight so that it cannot escape.

Thus, the Gelyant warrior with feline cunning attacked directly under the helmet of the Recruiter. Unlike the lioness, she attacked with the huge claws of her right hand, and with her left, she took his back. Agui's mother's bronze body crossed in front of the Recruiter, and in movements worthy of the best human gymnast, she pierced his throat. The helmet lay on his shoulders as the Recruiter's limbs gradually lost strength.

Then she let him go, and as she prepared to attack the one who accompanied him, causing trees to fall and caves to collapse, she glanced sideways as a powerful blue beam, which had previously come from one of Ebrom's weapons, floated, challenging gravity with the help of his transparent blue suit with silver contours. It approached quickly, and that blink helped her dodge it, though not without tearing the skin on her face.

Behind it emerged an explosion as it collided with the ground, sending the Gelyant's body forward. In the fall, the powerful Medrian with the Knolot suit flew at great speed and caught her by the neck with his left hand. Then he rose slowly, holding her, and the warrior's body moved without strength, while her head spun, trying to regain consciousness, as the explosion had severely stunned her.

"At last, I find you, Gelyant demon! Elusive as a mollusk, for such are trained all the females who deign to belong to the Gelyant race, the green planet of towering trees. Yet, I surpass you —not only in strength and speed, for with these Knolot weapons I clothe and shield my muscles, but in cunning, for I descend from true warriors, vile and invincible assassins who, in serving King Zetkorf, dared to defy the first possessor of the star, chosen by Amrok."

Thus spoke the Recruiter as he rose slowly above the trees, and during the ascent, Debki, with her thick hair, regained consciousness. Noticing that the Recruiter who had escaped her wrath, as Ebrom had prevented her from killing him like the previous one, was approaching —albeit unknowingly of the two candidates escaping. Her muscles stiffened to the point of exerting pressure on the hand that held her neck, attempting to make him let go.

However, Ebrom force was greater and did not set her free. Feeling cornered, she pointed her hand at the back of the Recruiter walking below, destroying trees. From her claws detached her hands as if fired from a high-powered rifle. They unfolded, breaking the air, and did not cease their path until one by one pierced the armor, which, despite being made of the strongest and most resistant material in the universe, was no match for the claws, since these fed on the most toxic foods produced by the Gelyant planet.

Once expelled, nothing stood in their way. They crossed like a knife heated in live embers piercing a bucket of butter, which not only melted but split apart. Astonished, the Recruiter turned his helmet toward where Ebrom was struggling with Debki in the elevated sky. He exhaled his last breath, his muscles went limp, and the suit that had trapped the whitish body of a Knolot collapsed.

"Reckless! You have already caused two casualties in the army that guards the universe and, in the service of King Perfidius, carries out his orders. For that, you will pay with your life, for only thus is it fair to grieve the dead, avenging those whose lives were taken by your hand!"

He said this not out of care for the lives lost but rather for the honor of the army. Such are the assassins who serve the dark intentions of the Medrians, relentlessly seeking to resemble the Creators. He squeezed the hand holding Debki by the neck, and the force of his muscles began to drain her strength.

Not far from there, Agui's honey-colored eyes filled with tears. The liquid coursing through her veins began to boil as if a pot of water were placed over the fire. Her thighs involuntarily moved forward, claws extended from her hands and feet like sharp knives, sharp teeth bared, and the hairs on her back and neck stood on end—not from cold but from anguish. She was ready to attack the Medrian Recruiter who was slowly taking the life of her mother, but Axel's prudent hand gripped her right arm.

Though he lacked strength, for the muscles of a warrior's daughter did not compare to those of a human, Axel spoke in a calm voice. "It is your mother who sacrifices for you, not the other way around. Though life is priceless, for one's destiny cannot be measured in gold, yours, in this case, is more valuable. Everything indicates, as your mentors say, that you will be the one to possess the star, and it will save millions. Even though today may break the last bond that ties you to the planet of your birth, what came before you will pass into history."

The young Gelyant wept, her tears growing thicker, and sorrow invaded her spirit. Her anger dissipated, and Axel's words found their mark. She looked to the sky, meeting her mother's eyes, and filled with love. The one defending life by gripping Ebrom's arm with both hands felt a brief electric shock that injected energy into her heart and limbs.

Three of her claws expelled from her left hand, striking and sinking into the Recruiter's arm covered with armor. He immediately let go. Even at more than twenty feet in height, Debki maneuvered with feline reflexes and despite her blurred vision, she managed to land on her feet. Without looking at her daughter or the human accompanying her, she smiled tenderly —a smile understood by all present— and fled as fast as her feet allowed, silently, fearing discovery.

"Better this way," Ebrom surprisingly said, descending slowly and shaking the arm left unprotected. Dark blood was invisible to Gelyant eyes as they awaited him in a defensive stance.

"Before killing you, I must extract information about your daughter's whereabouts. I omitted it earlier due to the rage that flooded my mind when I saw those who honorably wore the armor of the royal army dead. Now that you've freed yourself, your death will be more agonizing.

"Not only will I finish you off, but before eliminating you and sending your spirit to a reserved place in Medrian for the souls that belonged to the lives we took, I will rip the lives from the elders you protect and the useless Gelyant who comes with you.

"What a misfortune for your race that the male is merely an ornament, something that nature agreed upon. Still, I will take their lives before your eyes. And when I have your daughter, I will take her to King Perfidius to await her fate with the other candidates, as he seizes the Eye of Amrok once again."

This did not intimidate the warrior at all; on the contrary, she welcomed the idea of a fight. For one who fights by nature, pain is sweet, and threats only serve to cleanse the saliva from the lips.

Ebrom fired a blue ray from the weapon forming just above his left shoulder, which Debki easily dodged. But in doing so, she neglected her guard, and the Recruiter moved at a surprising speed —as fast as a blink if ab eye— appearing in front of her to strike her stomach with his good arm, forcing her to expel the air stored in her lungs. Then he struck her face, sending her flying toward one of the trees, which caught her body as it crashed into it.

The speed and strength of the royal assassin exceeded that of any previous opponent the warrior had faced while defending her planet and her people. And suddenly, she saw him again up close, smiling with all his sharp teeth. She showed no sign of pain; on the contrary, this angered the Medrian, who suddenly broke her legs and allowed her to fall to her knees while he held her long hair with the five fingers of his good hand.

"Now you will take me to the elders, or you will join those who, before you, have died by my hands," the leader of the Medrian army said, but his words didn't evoke any fear in Debki, who continued to laugh.

"Fine, if your wish is to die, I won't be the one to stop you. Anyway, the elders and your daughter shouldn't be far, and if I have to destroy this forest, I will —and them along with it.

Everyone will scatter like frightened animals from the smoke and fire consuming everything that dwells here.

"And I'll tell you something to etch into your memory: even when you are a spirit and your soul wanders in the vastness of the *Valley of Shadows* in Medrian, capable of remembering, it will be the same fate that awaits your planet and everything that lives in it."

Ebrom's armor removed its helmet, revealing his skin the color of the universe and his eyes, so blackly green that even the worst darkness couldn't compare. His woolly hair began to move slowly, and two strands shot out toward Debki. One embedded itself in her left shoulder, and the other in her heart.

The Medrian uttered inaudible words and, staring into her eyes, showed his snowy teeth. The lines of woolly hair tightened, causing intense pain to the Gelyant. This pain instilled fear —a terror she had never felt before, as if life were being snatched not only from her but also from her daughter and husband. She felt as though she were losing the life force from all three— the final thoughts, desires, and the will to live that precedes death.

Gradually, all her muscles lost strength, and what is known as the soul hovered above her body, which fell lifeless to the ground once the woolly strands merged back with the rest of Ebrom's hair.

"Go and join the others who supply energy and keep the first planet created within this universe in darkness. There will be terrors for you and great joy for those who inhabit it."

That's how Ebrom spoke, and the dark energy dispersed into the air. The blue suit with silver accents covered his face once again. Immediately afterward, he communicated with the Recruiters waiting in the ship, and five members clad in similar blue suits —some parts silver and arms in various places— descended. One took care of carrying the bodies of the fallen, and the others stayed with him to search for the remaining Gelyants within that tragic forest.

Chapter VIII

After leaving the young orphan, disoriented and in need of reaching that green forest, Ammy felt nostalgia and remorse. She had never been a mother —not for lack of desire, but time. She had devoted her life to journalism, always with the aim of informing the citizens, as she believed that society deserves to know the truth. To her, when the truth is known, lies become redundant, and society gains greater clarity for decision-making. At least, that's how she saw it.

She glanced in the rearview mirror, but Axel was no longer there. Only a couple of seconds had passed, during which she had moved no more than ten meters, and yet he had disappeared. She stopped the car and hurriedly got out, running barefoot toward the vast diversity of trees, shouting the name of the orphaned son several times without receiving any response.

Guilt invaded her thoughts and body; she had not taken care of him, despite being entrusted with the task. She sat on a recently cut log, contemplating the relativity of existence. For fourteen years, she had searched for any clue that would lead her to him. Now that she had found him, she realized she didn't want to be close. Her argument lacked coherence, yet now he was gone —just as he had been in the beginning— and she felt the need to search for him again.

The possibility of finding him seemed greater now. The forest was smaller than the planet, and the planet smaller than the universe, assuming the story she had been told was real. She wondered how deep into the forest she would have to go to find the truth and face uncertainty once more.

She contemplated for several minutes, whispering his name, then whispered the names of his father and mother, imagining them trapped among the shadows cast by the trees when the sun rises and before it sets. She felt a void in her stomach and remembered she hadn't eaten since the night before.

Silently, she moved her legs and rose, the wind blowing out of the forest, pushing her back toward the car. Once inside, she closed the door, adjusted the rearview mirror to point at the vehicle's gray carpeted ceiling, and pressed the accelerator. She didn't stop —there was no one to stand in her way. The roads were empty of cars, and she ignored the traffic lights, confident that any law enforcement officer wouldn't question the reasons for her hasty departure.

She joined Highway 81, heading back to New York. No one feels more secure than in their own city. She didn't fear unfamiliar streets or the local accent, and even if she only knew a few people there, she felt at home eating in restaurants or driving on the roads. The buildings were familiar, and she had grown accustomed to the smell and noise. For the city dweller, it was a unique kind of music.

Although she hesitated at first, as she was entering the city after driving for more than six hours, Ammy pulled out her mobile phone from her bag and called her old friend —technology expert and columnist at the same newspaper— Mark Demonte. The signal was interrupted, and she had no choice but to give up and keep driving, as she was close to his house. Nevertheless, she didn't want to arrive unannounced.

Her eyes signaled her brain, which, in turn, sent the order to press the brake with her left foot. All of this happened in a matter of milliseconds. The car skidded on the open road, veering from side to side until it came to rest sideways in the middle. Positioned as if pointing at 9:15 on a clock, Ammy couldn't take her hands off the steering wheel from the shock. Her limbs trembled as if the car's engine were beneath her feet.

Turning toward what had previously been the front but was now to the right, she recognized Mark. He was a young man with blonde hair, wearing black glasses, ripped jeans, and a white button-up shirt. Beside him stood a figure cloaked in a black tunic and hood that trailed on the ground. Thin lines of something resembling dark steel emanated from the hood, barely visible, like sunlight attempting to reach the pavement but colliding with itself. These lines extended toward one of the Recruiters floating clumsily in the air.

In front of them, another Recruiter struggled to stay afloat, trying to escape. Blue rays emerged from the Recruiter pierced by the dark metal strips, striking the suit of the fleeing one. It fell slowly.

Amanda Ríos got out of the car and began filming the scene with her mobile phone. The technology she witnessed was unlike anything she'd seen before, except in movies —and this was no Hollywood set. On her phone screen, she could see the blue and silver shine of the suit and the neon-like energy beams. These emerged from one Recruiter and struck another until it was defeated, crashing to the pavement with a sharp blow and leaving a large crater.

The figure in black drew the fallen Recruiter toward them, retracting the metal strips back into their head. When the two faced each other, the hood fell to the shoulders, revealing a loose hair that moved as if alive. The figure's skin was as dark as the universe, and their profile revealed human female features —a thin, pointed nose, nearly invisible, and eyes black as the depths of the sea with a faint greenish tone around the iris.

When they opened their mouth to speak, words inaudible to Ammy emerged, revealing pearly white teeth, like the whitest pearls on Earth. A dark gray cloud rose from the Reclaimer's armor, and when it dissipated, the suit remained motionless, floating with arms and legs extended. It moved parallel to the Medrian until it reached Mark, who nervously looked at Ammy.

"Take that one. There's no need to snatch his soul; he's already dead," the Medrian told Mark.

Mark didn't disobey, struggling to lift the Recruiter from the ground, though it weighed more than twice his own body. Ammy noticed as the Medrian and the lifeless Recruiter suit disappeared into Mark's house. Running, she called his name in a whisper:

"Mark! Mark!"

"Ammy? Is that you?" Mark replied, abandoning the suit and turning toward his co-worker. He hugs her with both arms, as if it had been a long time since they'd last met.

"It's good that you're here. Come on, put away your phone — turn it off preferably— and help me. My bones aren't that strong, and my legs falter trying to lift such weight," he said, downplaying the bewildered expression on her face.

"Wait, but what is this? Who is she? What is happening, Mark? You have to explain to me! I tried calling you, and there's no signal. The world is upside down, Mark!" exclaimed the experienced reporter, desperate and anxious, her voice trembling and saliva pooling excessively.

"It's not the world, Ammy; society no longer exists. Now chaos reigns from one end of the universe to the other, and it has shown its power on Earth so that there is no doubt —it has come to stay." Mark's gaze seemed distant, but his spirit remained intact. "Now, let's hurry inside. If they find us here, we'll be next to perish, and we've already lost many humans in a matter of days. Inside, I'll explain everything to you without omitting details so that your mind is awake, and your heart dictates your steps."

Somewhere in the crowded Bronx in New York, Mark and Ammy hurriedly carried the deceased Reclaimer. The body was so heavy that it made them sweat and groan during the more than fifty steps it took to reach the building's entrance. It felt like carrying an enormous tombstone while walking over a powerful magnet. The building's metallic structure seemed to pull their bodies downward, resisting their every move. Their muscles strained, and sweat oozed from every pore, as though they were lemons being squeezed.

When they finally crossed the wooden door of the building where they sought refuge, they immediately let go of the body. It fell to the floor with a thud that made the ground tremble, sending vibrations through the walls and their own bones.

Mark handed a black hooded cloak to Ammy, which hung by the entrance. Without waiting for an explanation, she put it on over her clothes, covering herself from head to toe as Mark had done. The cloak was heavy, though not as much as the lifeless body of the Reclaimer. Ammy exhaled under its weight, then took a deep breath and turned her attention to Mark, who was crouched beside the armor at their feet.

Mark hugged the armor with both hands, searching for a red switch located at the back near the waist. He found it quickly, moving with the precision of a seamstress threading a needle even with trembling hands. As the switch clicked, the full-body suit began to contract gradually, forming metal plates no larger than ten inches each. These plates accumulated on the chest —the upper ones folding down and the lower ones folding up— until they formed a compact metallic jumpsuit in blue, with a rectangular silver buckle at its center.

The buckle bore an image of the Knolot Scepter, now held by King Perfidius. Beneath the armor, the figure of a Knolot was revealed, dressed in a blue mesh suit with silver lines, dark lenses over the eyes, and an artificial breather connected to a hose leading to a box at rib height.

Mark snatched the suit and then covered the body with a dark fabric. As he lifted it, Ammy caught sight of at least three other lifeless bodies. Though the sight would shock most, it didn't frighten her. As an experienced reporter, she had faced similar scenes before. Despite the situation, she kept her focus on Mark, who took the armor and stored it in a similarly black box containing three others. He closed the box and turned to her with his intense gaze.

"Welcome to the end of the world," he said with a laugh, taking her hand and leading her toward the depths of the basement. The figure of the Medrian who had earlier ended the lives of two Recruiters disappeared into the shadows.

"Now, we'll wait for instructions from Trina. Please, don't be impatient. Oh, by the way, Medrians are peculiar; don't be afraid."

Against the wall, Amanda noticed Trina's pearly teeth gleaming as if smiling, though the figure remained still, waiting. Mark moved away slightly to approach the Medrian.

"This is Amanda Ríos. She works with me at the newspaper. Don't worry, she's trustworthy," Mark said nervously.

"I don't distrust humans. Though they possess willpower, they lack courage, making them a weak species. But don't worry about me. Go get her some food, feed her —she's come to your house, and hunger is evident in her eyes. Go alone; I have questions for her," Trina said, her tone commanding.

Without hesitation, Mark ascended the stairs to the kitchen, leaving Ammy and Trina alone. Women, as Trina believed, understood each other faster due to their liveliness.

"Where have you left the Earth candidate?" Trina asked once Mark was out of earshot.

"I'm not aware of his whereabouts. I left him where he indicated," Ammy replied cautiously.

"Your answer is clever, human, but I surpass you in years and wisdom. My species was the first created in this universe, the most similar to the Creator Amrok, who sees all. Do not limit your words, for it is not my intention to harm you but to help. Whether it is he, the other Earth candidate, one of the two Gelyants, or even the arrogant Knolots—whoever reigns over this vast yet finite universe will make Perfidius and the Medrians pay for their deeds. I am here to intercede for my planet and to achieve the harmony that Kendorf envisioned."

Trina's words carried determination, but they were alien to Ammy, who simply replied with a redundant phrase. Sensing her patience running thin, Trina decided not to press further.

"Very well. We will wait for them to appear and show us the way. Since you are stubborn and refuse to share what your mind holds, I will not use the *Potion of Truth*. It would force your spirit to bend, leaving your words devoid of falsehood. For now, rest and eat."

With that, Trina disappeared into the shadows of the basement, as if swallowed by the darkness. Moments later, Mark descended with a plate of soup, a piece of meat, and a loaf of bread.

Chapter IX

"Let's make way for evolution. Now we are part of a new society —a society that not only confines itself to living within a planet but travels through the universe at its leisure. This is the answer to many of the mysteries we have pondered for millennia. The integration of species is a reality. Once, we fought to unite all individuals —humans— and see ourselves as one, without discrimination. Now, we will do the same with the inhabitants of other planets.

The leaders of all nations forming this Earth have agreed that, over the next few years, we will work on building the bonds that keep us connected to the four species. This will be our contribution to the new universal order. The commander of the forces serving King Perfidius has assured us that there will be no further attacks threatening human lives as long as this integration treaty is fulfilled.

To achieve this, we have already taken the first step: the implementation of trackers. So far, we have progressed 99.9% —and I invite those who have not yet done so to join this social evolution. As a second phase, we have also agreed to allow extraterrestrial beings to enter our planet so that we can learn to live together and adapt to the changes. These beings will live with us, among us, and work in the same places. We will maintain social and economic rules, at least until King Perfidius orders otherwise."

The transmission echoed across all televisions, radios, mobile phones, internet pages, and every existing media outlet. The words were spoken by the President of the United States, who stood flanked by the leaders of other nations.

At his side, dressed in a recruiter's suit with his head uncovered, stood the Medrian commander Ebrom. His wispy hair, black eyes with green irises, pointed nose, alabaster teeth, and skin the color of the universe made him an imposing figure. He shook hands with the President as the speech concluded, greeting the audience watching from every corner of the planet.

"Oh, weak and innocent humans! You have surrendered to evil, thinking you were not negotiating with terrorists. You have fallen into the clutches of one who has them so sharp that, with a simple scratch, he will cut your intestines. However, I understand that you know you are overmatched. Your weapons are harmless against the recruiters and utterly useless against the immense power of the Knolot Scepter and the Amrok Star. The terror produced under Perfidius' hands is intentional, meant to cause harm."

Knolot Betokar's words were interrupted by John Flames, who had also heard the transmission on an analog radio.

"Do you think we are unaware of Perfidius' intentions, O mighty Betokar? Even you, who possess armor more powerful than any recruiter's, refuse to fight him head-on because he surpasses you in all aspects of combat —just as he does to anyone in this universe. It is not unknown to us. For years, we fought against someone with the same intentions. Although human, he threatened our kind.

But now it's clear we don't know how to defeat him, and our weapons are incapable of facing him. Trying to harm him only amuses him. So, go on —tell us the plan and why you are here. If it serves any purpose and we are of use, we will carry it out. We are still free from the cruel trackers that deprive the wearer of precious freedom, revealing everything about them."

So spoke the distressed John Flames, who had collaborated in Betokar's escape alongside the other Knolot candidate, Onruks.

"It is Onruks, candidate for the Eye of Amrok and citizen of Knolot, who must await his orders. He is currently searching for King Larks and gathering all the candidates he can to fight against the immense Perfidius. For now, we wait. When the time comes, Onruks will tell us what to do."

Betokar's reply was tinged with frustration. Known as a lover of war and battle, his greatest enemies were patience and strategy.

"Now, tell me, valiant John —who risked his life to rescue his beloved son and joined the fight against the unbeatable— why do you cling to this so-called freedom as if it were a precious treasure? Before this plague of Recruiters, you were subjected to countless systems and regimes. Even technological advances meant to ease your lives invaded your privacy.

What difference does a tracker make? It not only monitors but also forces peace, putting an end to the social disputes created to distract the lower classes. With the Recruiters' surveillance, there will be order. The human race will thrive —not only in knowledge but also in behavior and values.

Why don't you yield, as those who govern now understand? What makes you fight? The same will be done as before, but not empirically —practically. Beliefs and religions will be eliminated, and a just system will govern, as it does in Medrian, Knolot, and Gelyant. These laws transcend reason and morality, dignifying life and enhancing it, so long as one does not disobey the bearer of the Amrok's Eye or his army. It will be a prosperous life —a complete civilization."

"I omit none of what you've said in my decisions," John replied, "for each point you emphasize is correct, magnanimous Betokar. But because I now differ from your position, that's why I fight —because I can.

Perhaps this world and its rules are imperfect, but each of us is capable of choosing. It is this choice —even if an illusion created by those who command— that governs us. It is the power of choice that allows us to live with dignity.

Living is not only about serving and obeying, as those on the planets you mention do. It is about creating, deciding —and that's why I fight. That's why all of us here are willing to defend our planet and our laws."

"Your intentions may not be enough to fight such a vast and powerful army," Betokar conceded. "But if your heart commands it, I will not interfere with the path you choose. If fighting is what you desire, then we will fight. That is what we have been created for: to fight —even when the battle seems lost before it begins."

Both encouraged each other, brightening the spirits of those around them with their words. Ready to fight, they followed the instructions of the Knolot warrior, his golden-toned armor glittering with tiny silver particles that moved of their own accord to any part of his body. They trusted he had a strategy superior to the armies that had futilely defended Earth and were now being dragged into universal civilization.

However, while they faced adversity locked in the depths of that house, built with strong foundations and surrounded by metal plates, outside, in the streets —where ideas are not just discussed but applied— life appeared peaceful.

Though citizens remained watchful, their eyes constantly scanning the sky, waiting for what might come, they did not fully understand the implications of the warning from the President of the most powerful nation. Exhausted of resources, he had chosen to surrender to those who invaded and rapidly altered the social order.

This phenomenon wasn't limited to the streets of the United States; it extended across the globe. Even in nations once ruled by tyrants, where cruel armies abused power and kept citizens in submission —leaving them hungry and blind in both spirit and mind— peace now reigned.

The people, though frightened, emerged from their homes, finally tasting sustenance worthy of their existence. For those who had lacked so much for so long, the sudden abundance felt surreal. It was as if they had entered a dream where imagination provided nourishment, or perhaps they had transcended to the afterlife. Yet, they continued going to their workplaces.

For humans, the most challenging thing to uproot is habit —it becomes ingrained in memory and the body, much like an operating system absorbing and adapting, dictating daily rituals: waking, grooming, praying, working, smiling hypocritically, and living— even with a metaphorical collar replaced by a chip capable of remote destruction.

The new social system eliminated borders, integrating cities under one global structure. Recruiters worked tirelessly to dismantle all facilities capable of producing atomic or nuclear materials, fearing even the faintest spark of rebellion. Such weapons, proven useless against Ebrom's army and the Knolot Scepter, were now seen only as tools of self-destruction, no longer a means of liberation. The fear of annihilation kept the masses compliant; they saw no purpose in sacrificing more lives or resources.

As days turned into weeks, the massive explosions that once signaled the Recruiters' arrival began to fade from collective memory. Instead, humanity focused on adapting to this new, utopian society. The essentials —food, water, clothing, shelter— were provided to all. The system of government shifted from democracy to autocracy, with Ebrom assuming the role of an emperor.

This transformation was orchestrated by Ebrom's media strategy. His team of skilled communicators flooded every screen and device with messages of peace, harmony, and glimpses of life on Knolot. These futuristic images captivated Earth's inhabitants, presenting an alternate reality that many saw as paradise —the fulfillment of religious promises of eternal life. Conspiracy theories emerged, drawing connections between extraterrestrial life and earthly messiahs, but no tangible evidence ever surfaced.

• • •

Mark, lost in thought, finally looked up at Amanda. His eyes, heavy with exhaustion, reflected the burden of having witnessed too much in too little time.

"What's happened, Mark? It's been barely sixty days, and the entire world has forgotten the devastation brought by that army. Now, they track and deprive every inhabitant of freedom. Worse, they flood our cities with other species, without consent, under the guise of unity. Colonizing is not the same as fraternizing. Why have journalists relinquished their power, handing the eyes and ears of the world to Ebrom?"

From the dimly lit basement of Mark's home, Amanda Ríos voiced her frustration. Weeks without practicing her profession and being confined to brief excursions had left her restless. She waited, as always, for Trina's elusive instructions.

Mark, his expression weary, moved closer, his uncertainty mirroring Amanda's own.

"Amanda, the world has fallen into a kind of lethargy —a collective amnesia that seems to have clouded humanity's memory. We don't know what dark force has enveloped everyone, journalists included, in this shroud of indifference and acceptance. Reality fades among the shadows of the unknown."

Mark's attempt to explain the inexplicable trailed into a melancholic silence that echoed in the basement. Amanda's eyes, filled with unease, clung to the little certainty they had left, yearning for answers in a world where questions seemed to dissolve into the silence of complicit days.

"How naive all of you are," said Trina the young Medrian, emerging from the shadows that had concealed her. Shrouded in her robe, she had remained invisible to Amanda and Mark until now.

"You have never thought for yourselves. You believe you have, but you haven't. The so-called freedom you speak of has been stolen from you since you existed as a society —it was taken from you at birth. You are subject to so many norms, and Perfidius knows this well; his knowledge is infinite. Carrying the eye of Amrok, the creator of universes, he studied you even before the appearance of the Recruiters, long before you existed as a society. Ignorance is not only the absence of knowledge but also the absence of experience.

"You have been colonized by one who possesses all knowledge, and it hasn't been difficult for him to use it against you. When he attacked with tremendous weapons to demonstrate his power, he instilled fear in your minds, showing you how impossible disobedience would be. He surpasses you in technology; your earthly weapons are useless against his army. However, fear alone is not the tool to control humans. I realized that as soon as I arrived here —and he knew it long before.

"So, he gave you hope. He didn't take anything from those who already have, for they control the masses. He kept the economic and governmental systems intact, allowing you to feel as though you're still in control. This desperate need for control leads you to surrender without resistance, to sacrifice everything you hold dear in exchange for an illusion of power —a vain illusion that fills your minds. Still, he gave power to those who had nothing. He opened the borders, redistributed food, and offered prosperity.

"But that is not the key to his conquest. Forgetting millions of deaths, erasing pain from human minds, is a simpler task. All it takes is keeping people entertained with symbolic distractions. He promised you countless things, and I am sure he will fulfill them to the letter. By gaining your trust, he gains time and slaves. To achieve this, he launched a massive media campaign because a single message convinces no one. It might move them, but repetition —that is his weapon. Repetition suppresses memories, ideas, and desires for revenge in human minds.

"The hope of living for many years, almost to immortality, is an attractive offer for those who lived on this planet in past generations. Yet, if you live in a society ruled by his imposed system, every day —every terrestrial year— becomes immortal, for each hour is the same. Those who once had their own lives will become automatons. That is what you face now, and that is why those who rebel against this conquest choose to fight."

And she submerged herself in the shadows again, having answered all the doubts of the two humans sharing the same space as her.

"What's the difference with the world now?" mumbled the technology columnist, looking and exchanging glances with his companion. The latter remained seated and silent for several seconds until she looked away, feeling overwhelmed by the information. Ammy then answered with a broken spirit and tears on her cheeks, as if hope were dying in front of her, shattering as it fell to the ground.

"It will be for a longer time," replied the blogger, and both fell silent, pondering on what was said. They sat in front of a plate containing canned food and bottled water.

"Feed your body, for it seems your soul has been ripped away. It is time, we are going in search of Larks. It's time to begin the fight," Trina broke the pessimistic silence, and after this, there was no word for the consecutive hours. The revelation had opened a door in their minds that was impossible to close, casting doubt on what was previously known. But the spirit injected by the battle warmed their bodies and blood, just like the soup they drank from their plates.

Chapter X

They had traveled for twenty nights until they reached San Antonio, Texas. They took refuge across from the AT&T Center, in an abandoned warehouse that had once served as storage for industrial paper rolls. In the lifeless space, rust peeled from layers of old paint on dormant machines. Axel removed his coat, and the fluorescent blue light emitted by the lines on his legs and hips illuminated the surroundings.

After a brief inspection, they settled in a corner where the windows faced the outside. In front of them, a crowd had gathered, indicating that the match between the Spurs and the Lakers was in full swing. Life for humans had seemingly continued undisturbed, despite their existence now being marked and monitored as though livestock on a farm. Even with the knowledge that they were not alone in the vast universe, humans sought the comfort of routine.

This belief, shaped by society since time immemorial, had created both wonder and uncertainty about what lay beyond Earth. However, the unprecedented media campaign —collaborating with authorities and the Recruiter army led by Ebrom— had dulled the horrors of the last two months. Now, confidence was returning; people walked the streets, attended events, and resumed their lives, striving to forget so as not to remember —a cycle where both acts meant the same thing.

From the warehouse, Agui watched the crowd with her honey-colored eyes. She had momentarily distanced herself from Axel, her travel companion and destiny's co-conspirator. Both had been chosen to meet —not necessarily in this place, but somewhere in the vast universe and at this precise time— to fulfill a shared mission. Preparing food had become her daily task since their departure from the Allegheny National Forest, a routine she repeated faithfully. Axel patiently waited during the day, though he grew restless as the night wore on. They hid in forests, abandoned buildings, or wherever they could, only stopping to eat and recover.

Outside, the sun glinted off the canopies of parked cars, casting a brilliance that forced passersby to don sunglasses. Yet, even in their shaded view, everyone occasionally glanced toward the sky. Despite repeated assurances of "normalcy" and "progress," fear lingered. The persistent dread that something might fall from above and erase their existence was unshakable. Agui noticed this and whispered her observation to Axel, who was engrossed in his meal.

The food prepared by Agui, a young Gelyant, was unlike anything Axel had ever tasted. It awakened his senses as no meal ever had. When he first sampled the dried meats and spiced leaves, he questioned the concept of freedom itself. The sheer delight of the flavors made him reconsider everything he'd learned on Knolot. It felt as if a new dimension had been revealed to him, one where his senses ruled supreme, free and unshackled.

Yet he quickly realized that dependence on such pleasure rendered him a prisoner once more. "You're only free before and during the moment of indulgence," he mused, discarding the thought to savor the meal uninterrupted.

"What are we doing here?" Axel asked after finishing his meal and approaching the window where Agui stood.

"We're fleeing."

"From what?" Axel looked perplexed.

"From the past."

"It's impossible to escape the past," Axel countered. "Our encounter with it is inevitable, especially since it never truly ceases to exist. The past reigns over the universe, and no matter how hard we try to leave it behind, it will always find us."

"No," Agui replied. "Not if we find it first. That's why we're heading toward it."

"I don't understand."

"The past has many faces. Don't worry, you never will. It's your human condition that limits you."

"Is that why we stopped in this city?"

"I thought you meant the planet," Agui retorted, her eyes fixed on the crowd outside. A foreboding sense crept into her, sharpening her instincts. She gripped Axel's forearm with her clawed hand, embedding her sharp nails into his skin to prevent him from bolting.

The crowd outside scattered abruptly, like ants disrupted at mid-trail. Bewildered, they ran in opposing directions —some to the right, others to the left. A few spun in place as though lost, while others retraced their steps back toward their cars. Chaos unfolded before the AT&T Center as two Knolots emerged and began firing into the crowd with weapons designed by humans themselves.

The Knolots wore black-striped uniforms, resembling those descending from the ship yet not part of the Recruiter's army. They seemed like prisoners on this planet. Both wore dark glasses covering their blue eyes and respirators connected to their hips, allowing them to survive in Earth's atmosphere.

One of them, taller than the other, wore, besides the dark glasses as dark as night, an external lens that granted him vision beyond what any common Knolot could possess. He seemed to be in control, wielding an AK-47 and firing without hesitation. The other, bulkier but shorter, carried not only an AK-47 but also a bazooka on his left shoulder and a belt with grenades strapped across his chest.

Faced with such atrocity, Axel felt the urge to rush to the scene, but he was stopped by Agui's firm grip on his right forearm and the enhancers embedded in his lower limbs.

"I share your anger," said Agui, her voice calm yet resolute. "And since what my eyes see is unjust, I agree that we must defend those defenseless ones who flee and perish at the hands of these wicked Knolots. I must confess, though, that it surprises me to see you react with such human impulses, as you have neither been educated nor induced to feel this unity. But I believe that gallantry is imbued in your genes. After all, you are the son of a warrior."

"As you are too," Axel retorted. "More surprising is my restraint —not attacking while talking. From what I've seen, Gelyant warriors enjoy this more than anything else. Why have you stopped my impulse when my desire is to fight and defend those who can't do it themselves?"

"You're wrong, Axel. Humans are capable of defending themselves against Knolots, Medrians, or Gelyants. Any of them would be just another war. What they can't do is stop Perfidius with all his power. No one is immortal, but whoever bears the Eye must understand this: there will be no time when death is near, and escape is impossible.

"Now, due to the rules implemented by Ebrom, they are vulnerable. They lack weapons to fight injustice, and the Knolots have taken advantage of this situation. So let's go, but let's be stealthy. Despite my warrior blood, remember that I am a candidate to possess the kingdom of the universe.

"Therefore, I am trained in many arts —patience being one of them, cunning another. Let's get as close as possible to those who disturb our imposed peace, and when we're close enough, use the strength of your enhancers to throw a car at them. This will distract them, and then they'll meet my fury."

So wisely spoke Agui, and although Axel found her words a bit arrogant, he did not disobey, for her wisdom surpassed his.

They stealthily exited the building. When they were close enough, Axel kicked a lightweight vehicle with his enhanced legs, sending it crashing into the smaller Knolot. The impact hurled him into the glass walls of the AT&T Center, breaking at least five panels before slamming into a counter. Dazed, he struggled to get up.

The commotion distracted the taller Knolot, who began shooting indiscriminately toward the direction the vehicle had come from. Taking advantage, Agui lunged at him, embedding her claws into his chest. Spinning, she lifted him over her shoulders and hurled him toward his companion, who was still recovering.

For a moment, the fleeing crowd, terrified and desperate, paused to witness the strange figure of a young woman with a curved back, long limbs, and extended arms throwing the pale-skinned alien into his semi-conscious comrade. Some cheered and applauded before continuing their frantic escape, like a current flowing away from a waterfall. But the force dragging them was not gravity —it was fear and the memory of devastation.

Agui turned to Axel, who smiled, encouraged by the cheers. But the moment of triumph was short-lived. The wind carried a grenade from the Knolot's hands, and its explosion hurled Agui's body into a parked vehicle. The impact dented the metal and left her unconscious, her muscles limp and the light fading from her eyes.

Distraught, Axel leapt toward her. With two long strides, he closed the distance, cradling her in his arms. Though unfamiliar with the act of care, he instinctively supported her head. Remembering a technique his father had taught him during their brief journey to Earth, he felt for a pulse on her jugular. She was alive but weak. He carefully laid her down, aware that danger loomed. A second grenade exploded, thrown haphazardly by the recovering Knolots.

The two Knolots, now steadied, began walking toward Axel and the unconscious Gelyant. Though they could have shot from afar, they chose not to. Revenge, they believed, was more satisfying up close.

When they were near, the taller Knolot, spoke. "You Fool! Why do you dare attack those who surpass you in experience and knowledge? From afar, the glow of your enhancers deceived me into thinking you were a Knolot. But now I see you're just a human, influenced by the ethics of that Gelyant lying there.

You must have acted out of misplaced heroism, interpreting our actions as unjust. But tell me, what value does a life condemned to eternal obedience have? You won't answer, for humans and Gelyants alike have always been slaves —to beliefs or customs. Still, I'll ask one more question, as your answer will add meaning to your death: who are you, and what are you doing here? Your technology is ancient to us, yet undeveloped on Earth."

So spoke the Knolot who called himself Carzo when he stood in front of Axel. "Who I am is none of your business; however, what I do here, I think, doesn't need explaining, as you've already said. One who values life cannot take it away. However, unscrupulous beings who prioritize science over Amrok's creation and take what does not belong to them must fear revenge, for it is the only price that compensates for such foolishness," replied Axel, standing next to his inert friend.

"The Gelyant double morality —I see your companion has infected you with it. Your brain is so primitive, and therefore, your reasoning. Science, oh naive human, lacks morals because it does not belong to life; life belongs to it. It is this lack that guides societies and species to progress, as it does not stop with such banal aspects as ethics.

"The survival of the species is more important than the singular being. That's why planets like this and Gelyant lag behind while Knolot and Medrian surpass and submit them with such ease. They fear us and run when they see us; they get scared when we do them the favor of taking away their lives, as life is so insignificant to them that it doesn't matter if they have it or not."

Axel answered with few words: "What you disdain so much is what keeps you standing and opens your eyes. Yet arrogance blinds your soul —if indeed the Knolots were endowed with such a quality. Perhaps they've convinced you otherwise on your planet, as they have the ability to create illusions and imprison the senses, exchanging freedom for control by instilling and spreading fear in beings with noble souls.

"But know this —you are mistaken. It is not freedom but repression, and oppressed masses always have the advantage of at least thinking about freedom. When this thought emerges, those, like you, who feel intellectual superiority suffer the consequences. And as now, in pain, you move clumsily, so shall you depart from this universe."

"The audacity you speak with! Surely, you are driven by fear, for you know that death is near, and boasting in front of your assailants may confuse the weak. But as I've said before, we surpass you in so many ways that I wouldn't finish naming them. And seeing that your courage doesn't wane but fear injects you with vigor, it's better to quell it.

"Though primitive, it's most accurate to do so with these weapons that cannot compete against ours. But not being in Knolot, it's better than having nothing. I will take your life and then do the same with the young one you try to protect by taking steps forward."

When Carzo finished speaking, Axel understood he had to act. If he could at least distract the two Knolots, he might save Agui.

"Does this mean being human?" he wondered. "Compassion for others."

But there was no time to ponder this enigma. He decided to lunge forward, toward Carzo. If he managed to knock him down, he would try to run, and they would follow him, leaving Agui behind. As he prepared his legs for the leap, a "biped" emerged from the back of Cretn's neck. At the sound, a flickering blue light —the same blue as Axel's enhancers— began to intensify. Cretn panicked.

"What's happening, Carzo?" he said in a rough, raised voice.

"It is necessary that you flee, Cretn. Run far and don't try to come back, for it is for you that the Recruiters are coming." Carzo answered with fear in his voice.

Hearing this, Axel noticed the two Knolots arguing about whether to stay together or separate. It was then that he seized the opportunity. Taking Agui's unconscious body in his arms, he propelled himself with all his might, using the enhancers to escape the place.

Carzo noticed this, albeit belatedly, and began firing the AK-47, the bullets riddling vehicles they passed but failing to hit Axel in time. From the sky descended, like lightning in an electrical storm, two Recruiters, their presence severing Cretn's prudence.

Cretn, burly, grabbed Carzo's arm and dragged him inside the AT&T Center, though Carzo shouted imperatively for him to let go. Cretn didn't listen —terror blocked his ears. The flashing light and the "beep, beep, beep" sound echoed throughout the basketball stadium. Spectators, initially annoyed by the commotion, threw soda cans, popcorn, and beer cups from the stands. But when Carzo detonated his weapon, chaos erupted, and people took cover behind their seats.

The sound was deafening. The Recruiters destroyed the roof of the sports center, sending glass, rocks, and metal crashing down. They landed in the middle of the court, shaking the entire structure. The two Knolots fired desperately at the blue-armored figures with silver veins, but their weapons could not penetrate the armor forged on Knolot.

The Recruiters soon captured them. First, they struck their stomachs, leaving them breathless and powerless. Then, they disarmed them, grabbed their feet, and slammed them against the court floor, mimicking the basketball game that had been interrupted moments before.

Axel managed to carry Agui to the refuge where they had planned to spend the afternoon before becoming embroiled in the tragic dispute. He laid the inert body of the young Gelyant on the warehouse floor and looked out the window. From there, he saw a blue light burst from the AT&T Center, shattering the roof completely. Beyond the explosion, the two Recruiters emerged, holding Carzo and Cretn in their grasp. The Knolots struggled as they were carried through the sky, vanishing from Axel's sight and that of the crowd below.

The citizens dispersed as Ebrom's message flashed on the world's screens, declaring an intolerance toward evil and the disruption of public order. He exalted the punishment awaiting the two Knolots—being left in space with enough air to survive for five hours, only to die of asphyxiation in the vast emptiness. To many, it was an exemplary punishment.

Chapter XI

Agui awoke with the dawn of the next day, a sign that they would wait at least all morning. They had lost a night, and spirits were shattered —especially for the young Gelyant, whose body bore the invisible marks of the explosion and the car. Bruises hid beneath the dense layers of golden fur covering her skin, but they did not escape the senses.

Axel, on the other hand, seemed bewildered, lost. Carzo's reflections on life and reason had confused him. Moreover, they hadn't eaten, as Agui was in charge of that and had been indisposed.

The night before, Axel had contemplated continuing with the green planet candidate in tow but hesitated. Anyone who doesn't know where they are going cannot continue without guidance. All he would achieve was further delaying the journey or getting lost —something acceptable for a human prone to mistakes.

However, it wasn't convenient, as he would drag someone who was not to blame for wasting their time, especially when time is all they have, and it was very little. So, he decided to wait for Agui to recover. While doing so, he looked outside and observed how everything returned to normal.

Four Recruiters arrived at the scene a few hours after the altercation with the two rebellious Knolots. They took less than an hour to reconstruct the AT&T Center, as if destined to erase the event from the memory of the inhabitants and implant the belief that it had never happened —masking reality or creating another.

Axel watched them the entire time, then saw how people passing by doubted that anything had occurred. Even if they had seen it on the news and the internet, their minds told them that maybe it was just part of the propaganda for a product or a science fiction movie. They walked or drove by until, later, they paid no attention.

Night fell with all the city lights, and some stars managed to escape the smoke clouds and urban glow. With it came the noise; the city's life on weekends begins when the moon arrives. Axel had never been on this planet, let alone in a place like this. The passive behavior of the people seemed normal to him. Cars always advanced, respecting speed signs, and pedestrians moved from one side to another without bothering those next to them. No one walked faster than another —a perfectly directed symphony by the orchestra conductor.

"How do you feel?" Axel asked.

"That is an unnecessary question, don't you think?" Agui replied. "The answer is implicit in the facts. However, not to seem impolite, I confess that I am very sore. I have fallen many times from very tall trees, but always landed on my feet or with the possibility of recovering. However, the explosion caught me by surprise. Incredible what weapons can do to modify nature and defy the laws by which planets are governed. Come, help me get up. It is my duty to prepare food to regain strength and move on in the night —even if slowly. At least we won't waste time waiting."

The young Gelyant walked a bit away from Axel, carrying the backpack.

"Where are we going?" Axel asked, anxious and expectant, as the food lifted his spirits and erased his doubts.

"To the south. We'll arrive in a couple of days," Agui replied, with pain in her voice and grunts in her movements.

Minutes later, she returned with two plates full of hot soup, herbs, and some other foods not regularly harvested on Earth. They existed, but humans had not noticed them.

Betokar began to speak in a low voice; John and the others, exercising their bodies to entertain their minds, listened attentively. They had been locked up for over six weeks, always waiting. Although one might think that life slips away in waiting, time moves on one direction only, and while waiting, it only walks forward.

They couldn't do anything else. Things in the city were worse —and "worse" doesn't always mean chaos. But we must first understand what normal or better means. In this case, "worse" translated to complete calm and the control of the aggressive human behavior through interference with their nervous system and the alteration of fear. Fear came from the sky and fell in the form of Recruiters, already destroying millions. The calm only disrupted the order of society and exposed that stepping out of such order was acceptable.

And this was done very well by John and James, old war veterans specialized in military tactics, intelligence, and counter-revolution. Instincts impregnate memory, and they react according to circumstances. Even if pressed voluntarily, they always emerge and darken the light with which one lives daily. It is impossible to disobey instincts, just as it is with physiological needs.

They only listened to what he said, as they were aware that Knolots could communicate through one of those chips installed at the back of the neck. Not telepathically, but with their own will to move objects and talk among themselves. Evolution, they insisted, was to develop technology that did the things intelligent beings preferred to avoid and this meant any movement involving body fatigue.

They also knew about the wait and Onruks' warning regarding the location of the former king of the universe, Larks, who had preceded the terrible Perfidius and was now exiled on Earth, monitored by the royal guard. He was known as the Guardian of the Sea, as they suspected Larks was hiding in a watery place. Onruks confirmed this suspicion, and when the conversation —crafted with whispers and neck movements— ended, Betokar addressed them.

Allegorically, he armed himself with his golden armor, over which silver points ran as if alive and moving of their own will.

It's time! But it is understandable that those unprepared for battle stay behind. Fear will cloud their consciousness, and if it surpasses their will, it will result in unnecessary loss of life. The mission would be doomed to failure, and their existence would have been not only in vain but also useless, just like their death.

Our weapons surpass those of any being in this universe. The only one capable of facing us is Ebrom, the Medrian, who possesses dark powers unknown even to the wise Knolots. Covered by a Recruiter's armor, he becomes invincible. This means that you would only be a hindrance in such a confrontation, should it take place.

However, one must never underestimate the audacity of a human and the strength of a brave heart —capable, as I have heard, of moving mountains. So, friends, if any of you waver in your intention to continue, do not hesitate —step out of the vehicle. It will be better for everyone.

Everyone listened, attentive to every word that echoed in the waiting room for Onruks' resolution. John was the first to put on the bulletproof vest and his camouflaged suit, preparing for war. Arthur and James followed suit. However, Leonor, the wife of the latter, felt nervous and fearful. Despite training with the others while they were desolate, she lacked enough experience and ingrained instincts to face such an enemy.

She walked away with her husband to a corner of the room, and after a few minutes, both notified the team of their decision. Everyone agreed, although they had thought about it beforehand, they hadn't expressed their thoughts for fear of hurting the feelings of the brave lady. Betokar saw this as a weakness because compassion breeds poor decisions, which multiply once the first is made.

With restored confidence, the team of three veterans and one surgeon prepared for the journey.

"We will head south. There is a river that originates and feeds into a vast ocean. There's an entrance to the heart of the sea. Onruks will see us once we get there. However, he has warned me that it's better to proceed by human means since the air is monitored constantly, and my presence would disrupt the order. So, load all your equipment into the car, and let's drive. Bring enough food for two days —that's how long it will take to get there by these means. And don't forget to pack courage; you'll need it."

Betokar spoke as everyone packed their war backpacks, filling them with enough ammunition to sustain a local battle for at least five days and cause the destruction of an entire city.

Once in the car, they decided on the drivers' shifts. Seeing Betokar shake his head, everyone agreed he would drive the last stretch from San Antonio to the Rio Grande Valley. It turned out to be a fiasco. Two tires deflated, and the car's body was dented from collisions with posts and road safety fences.

Laughter echoed among the humans traveling with him, initially provoking his anger. However, he realized he was in the presence of the human natural relaxant and encouraged the laughter. He even caught the gesture himself, as it spread like a virus from one person to another, regardless of species.

• • •

Agui suffered from dehydration, and Axel struggled to keep her awake. The food had run out the night before, when they devoured the las121t of their reserves —strips of some strange plant grown in the Allegheny National Forest in Pennsylvania. It had kept their stomachs calm, but as the sun completed its cycle, tempers frayed. Mood is the first casualty when food is lacking, for there is no happiness without it, and friendships rarely last unless a piece of bread or meat is shared.

Nevertheless, the young orphan carried Agui on his shoulders, as the Gelyant had not fully recovered. They hoped that upon reaching King Larks, he would relieve them with his vast wisdom.

It took them four hours to travel from San Antonio to Brownsville, Texas, a remote city hugging the sea. The salt clung to their cheeks, stirred by the wind, and the sun beat down harshly. The humid air caused the human body to swell, conditions that affected those not born on this soil the most. Conditions on other planets were nothing like this, but here, gravity reigned, making it impossible to escape the bad weather or the intense heat of the sun and sand stinging their eyes.

Agui led Axel to the place where the river begins, right on the seashore —where one world ends and another begins. But only for those who refuse to live like others, anchored to the earth, and instead see with their souls. At the river's mouth, the sense of location is lost, and doubts arise about the position of the being. Where does it head? Does its heart point upward or to the right? The gaze is drawn to the vastness and reflection. Axel experienced this for the first time and was tempted, like Narcissus, to lose himself in the enchantment, but the waves moving under the sun made him sick.

"Come on, it's this way!" Agui distracted him, leaning on his neck, her dangling feet scratching the relentless grass, unsupervised and untamed.

They headed to a huge stone by the sea, shapeless and with a volume similar to that of three stacked cars. Gently, Axel let the young Gelyant down, and once on the ground, both pushed the deformed rock as hard as they could to the right.

The wind helped them a bit, blowing cool, chasing away the heat like a vulture stalking the dying in the desert. After three attempts, they cleared a hole half a meter in diameter, large enough for both to fit comfortably. Their bodies, slender and tiny like the trunks of young trees, seemed insignificant compared to the universe that supported them.

Upon entering the cavern, they noticed the sun was blocked by the stone —the same stone that Trina would make levitate with the help of her hair, and later Betokar would destroy with a blue ray expelled from his golden suit.

"That light is enough to illuminate the path," Betokar had once said, arguing that it would be the last time anyone entered this place after they rescued King Larks from the hands of the Guardian of the Sea. The blue light illuminated the porous, fibrous path surrounded by walls of volcanic rock, which had floated to this place from distant regions. No one knew for certain, as no one had seen beneath the earth when such a massive stone blocked the way.

They advanced slowly. Axel removed his coat, no longer needing to keep up appearances in the depths of the earth, where prejudices cease to exist, and defects become virtues.

Axel avoided continuing the conversation, preferring not to argue with Agui, who was tired. He wanted to help her conserve energy. Besides, he assumed that if the conversation continued, he would have to tell her what he had seen. It would be worse for her to know, for absence isn't always physical and it's enough for a thought to wander for a person to cease to exist.

When they reached the end of the dark cave, visibility remained constant, illuminated by the enhancers on which the young orphan leaned. What once irritated him now saved his life, as Agui's sharp claws sank into his skin, tearing his clothes at shoulder height. She clung to him tightly to prevent his body from falling into the depths below.

With Agui's help, Axel managed to hold on and climb quickly. Adrenaline surged through his veins, his pulse racing, and his arteries filled with burning flames. He rubbed his bleeding shoulders. Though they hurt, the pain didn't stop him from breathing or trying to recover from the shock.

He jumped forward with both legs, and after a moment, they watched as a line of stone formed, covering almost the entire diameter of the empty circle before them. That line rotated as the Earth's clockwise does, balancing the time of the sea storm —a delicate interplay of gravity and inertia.

There was a gap between them and the line. As it rotated slowly, Agui grabbed the sore, reddened shoulders of the illuminating one once more, and without thinking twice, he jumped as if his life depended on it. Though he cared little about losing it —for, in his view, life lacked meaning— the impulse placed them on top of the stone line. It continued its course, seemingly unaware of the presence of those invading its rhythm. But when has time mattered to those going up or down, left behind or waiting impatiently?

Axel and Agui fell sideways, both in pain and with the last reserves of spirit stored inside them. Once again, they stood up. Limping forward, no one could deny that they were progressing. They moved in the direction their gaze pointed, but doing so on a spinning line meant little. This did not dampen their spirits; they had too little left to waste, so they kept moving.

At the very center of the circumference —that point that rotates "on its own axis"— a white light combined with the distinctive glow of Axel's enhancers and the Recruiter suits, blue, illuminated the space entirely. There, a perfect female figure appeared, human in form, as though sculpted by the hands of Phidias. Her body shimmered with sapphire, seemingly extracted from the same ocean, and in the center of her chest, like a pulsating heart, glowed a radiant white light resembling the moon.

The line of stone rotated around her, anchored by a massive pillar that extended downward, where water collided with it and with the walls of the concave cave.

"Only three candidates, despite there being five," said the Sapphire Guardian, her snowy light extending from her chest and emerging from her mouth like an exhalation.

As the two young orphans walked, they held hands. Agui stretched out her right hand, squeezing Axel's left. Despite the pain coursing through his body, Axel leaned on her without hesitation.

They didn't understand the meaning of the Guardian's words, but they saw her speak. The stream of light that illuminated the cave's sky like a lighthouse at a harbor's edge betrayed her speech, announcing to sailors that there was land.

The Guardian reached out to them, and they stopped, though beneath them the bridge kept moving. From the invisible depths of the cave, the water began to stir. Waves formed despite the lack of wind. The pillar that held the stone bridge —symbolizing time and the storm of the sea— remained unmoved. Its stillness defied the force of the waves, unbalancing nothing.

Two figures emerged from the water: a triton and a mermaid. Humanoid in shape, both were covered in scales. Their feet were webbed, and their backs were adorned with shark-like fins proportional to their bodies. The triton carried a metal trident, and the mermaid revealed large, pointed teeth.

"Kill them all!" ordered the Guardian, her voice directing light from her mouth toward the cave's exit. There, cloaked in shadows and long robes, reporters Rios and her companion, Mark, observed the scene. Each carried a backpack resembling a giant hump. Behind them, though completely invisible, Trina's green eyes gleamed.

The triton raised the trident vertically and aimed it at Axel. A faint ray of white light emerged, and if Trina hadn't positioned herself in front and caught the ray in a glass jar, it would have struck Axel, leaving his muscles powerless.

But not all were good news. In the process, the young Medrian made a sadistic movement, pushing Axel toward the shore. He dragged Agui with him, but sensing the imminent fall, Axel let go of her hand and plunged into the void.

"Axel!" Agui and Amanda shouted simultaneously.

"There's the fourth candidate!" the Guardian said as she grabbed the triton by the neck and slammed him with such force that, had he been human, he would have died in seconds. But as a triton, he only rose in pain.

"How can you be so inept? This proves why your species is extinct and humans control the world!" she exploded in anger.

Agui watched as Betokar soared at full speed toward the dark and invisible abyss, intent on saving John's son from the fall. John, standing at the cave's exit alongside the two reporters, watched helplessly.

"What was that?" asked Ammy and John, in good spirits and confidence as they knew him. They were told not to worry —Axel was in good hands.

"Have you seen the triton and the mermaid?" the reporter asked. "I thought those only existed in mythological tales."

"And being invaded by beings from other planets is also mythological," Mark interrupted.

The Guardian interrupted: "Human, so narcissistic egocentrism, which, even when they are brought to their knees, prevents them from opening their minds and eyes. All the signs appear in front of them, yet they doubt; some still believe they are dreaming.

"When those clock hands they stand and complete the full turn, the Eye of Amrok will have decided who will care for it. As predicted by King Perfidius, all of you are here, and even if the star chooses you, it will be too late for anyone to claim it; then he will live forever, and you will be claimed as energy to increase his power."

She smiled fully, and the light spun in all directions as she moved her head aimlessly.

"Do you speak of time, insolent Guardian, have you not realized that death stands before you? Although I doubt you understand its meaning —for you are not alive, not even truly existing— you are merely here as a hologram moved by the power of Perfidius. An existence that will cease when this hand completes a cycle," Trina interrupted, her black hair, like the universe, beginning to move in slow waves.

"Eliminate them all!"

Her breath broke as the words left her mouth. Though there was no signal, the urgency of the Guardian was evident as rocks fell behind the five humans sheltering under the tunnel, sealing their escape. Intermittent lights began to flash, accompanied by the sound of bullets. All were aimed at the scaly skin of the triton and the mermaid, but the impacts, while powerful, were ineffective. The creatures only stepped back slightly; their impenetrable bodies unaffected.

The time that passed while Trina positioned herself in front of the Guardian could be measured in the blink of an eye. Her sharp, black hair moved toward the sapphire embedded in the Guardian's chest. One by one, and then by the thousands, her strands —like diamonds— pierced the blue layer protecting the snowy light within. The Guardian felt no pain, but her eyes reflected the blackness of the Medrian and the primal fear of nonexistence. Even for one devoid of reason or soul, the fear of ceasing to be is overwhelming.

Trina's white teeth shone brighter with every millimeter her hair advanced. "Do not fear, Guardian! You will remain here when that clock completes its turn. I will use your energy to strengthen my weapons, and I promise you this: it will be with these weapons that I will snatch the Eye of Amrok and the life from your beloved King Perfidius."

"The most heinous crime is to corrupt your soul —to desire what the father possesses and not inherit it; but to kill him to gain it is more cowardly than parricide itself," said the Guardian, her words laced with an unsettling weight. No one could suspect the full meaning of such horrendous words.

Betokar emerged from the darkness, carrying Axel's limp body. Without strength, Axel lay motionless as Betokar gently placed him beside Agui. Then, turning his attention to the triton and the mermaid, Betokar activated his suit. The creatures, advancing with firm and deliberate steps, savored the prospect of revenge against humanity.

When Betokar stood before them, they claimed, "We will do neither good nor harm. These humans should perish, for they only hinder our task of recovering the Eye of Amrok."

But Betokar, resolute and strong of mind, refused to be persuaded. Without hesitation, he fired two blue rays from his arms, which transformed into cannons before returning to their original form. Both creatures fell into the water with a heavy splash, the sound of their motionless bodies breaking the silence of the calm sea.

Once they regrouped and checked their wounds, John cradled Axel, who was breathing slowly, while Ammy held Agui close. A deathly silence enveloped them; even the faint, lingering splash of the sea was absent. Only the creaking of the sapphire, slowly pierced by Trina's thin, strong hair, interrupted the stillness. The white light emanated from the Guardian's body through countless holes, casting beams in all directions.

"There is no escape, Guardian. Your life force will stay with me," Trina declared, her voice cold and certain.

Levitating the body of precious stone with her hair alone, Trina placed her hands in front of the radiant light. From her robe, she drew a container with a glass lid. Slowly, as if pouring liquid from a large jar to a small one, a constant stream of light began to flow, transferring the Guardian's life force into the container.

When the transfer was complete, Trina let the lifeless body fall to the ground. The sound of the shattering crystal echoed in the chamber, disturbing the silence like a glass vase breaking against stone. The resonance lingered in everyone's ears.

From the immovable midpoint emerged a glass container —a cell— holding King Larks. His skeletal body and snow-white skin, cloaked in a simple gray blanket from head to toe, revealed his frailty. Bald, like all Knolots, his long white beard covered his chin and lips.

Betokar moved carefully toward him, commanding his nanorobot suit to create an opening wide enough to extract Larks from the tiny cell. Placing his hand on the glass, the metallic particles shifted aside, shattering the barrier in seconds. Betokar gently lifted Larks, cradling him as a mother would a newborn.

"We need to get out of this place; Ebrom will not be long in arriving!" Larks said, his voice faint, like a thread of air.

Epilogue

The cavern sky opened as if woven with snow, allowing the sun to filter through. Onruks' suit, like Betokar's, gleamed with golden armor adorned with silver dots that moved autonomously across his entire body. These suits had contributed to building the rock chimney that led them toward the outskirts of the deep circumference of time itself.

Betokar recognized it immediately. With Larks in his hands, as if carrying a newborn devoid of strength, he emerged, sparks of silver trailing behind him and leaving everyone else behind. Onruks descended slowly, and upon seeing Agui for the first time, he couldn't look away.

Though he tried, embarrassedly, to turn toward the others, he found it impossible to stop observing those large, affectionate eyes and the smile that conveyed a sense of relief after enduring so much. It achieved nothing more than shattering his composure like sparkling glass.

He took Agui by the waist and held Axel by one arm. Axel, though conscious, was badly battered by the blows. Looking at Axel, Agui noticed Trina smiling beneath the darkness, ambitious and proud —like a Medrian consumed by arrogance. Behind Trina stood her father and everyone who had accompanied her.

Trina floated slowly over the hole, leaving the others. Though Mark and Ammy had arrived with her, they couldn't assist. She didn't stay to explain, simply levitating to cover the sunlight that had illuminated them.

Betokar returned, followed by Onruks after safely depositing those he had carried for the first time. They managed to rescue everyone: the doctor, the two soldiers, and the two reporters. Though humans, they were invaluable. After all, no one can win a war alone, especially in a foreign land. Wars are the same everywhere —the same concept of winner and loser, devoid of morality and perpetually confused with the notions of good and freedom.

Larks recovered quickly after receiving an artificial respirator from Onruks. He walked toward Agui, knowing that the Eye of Amrok needed to choose a Gelyant candidate. He examined her carefully, checking all vital signs. She was alive and would recover. With Knolot technology, no one alive can truly die —it's merely a matter of connecting them to nanorobots, which handle the process of rejuvenation. Both Agui and Axel, the most affected, were treated. Minutes later, they awoke, fully regenerated.

During their recovery, the three Knolots approached the humans, while Trina observed from the shadows.

"I see you have Recruiter suits," Onruks said, turning to Trina. "Surely it was you, wasn't it?" He avoided waiting for an answer; it was evident. Who else but her could have taken those four Recruiter suits?

"Then we'll proceed as follows: two brave soldiers, a Gelyant warrior, and one of you will wear them to fight. The doctor and the rest will provide support in case someone falls," Betokar interjected, silencing any friction caused by the Medrian.

"All right!" John said confidently. "It's time to start the war!"

"War, you say?" Onruks replied with a sardonic tone. "Oh, naive human! War exists only when the opponent has both the will and the power to fight. On this planet, the war was lost before the Recruiters even arrived. You are so innocent, with hope still lingering in your hearts. There will be no war —only a revolution. And revolutions, by their very nature, are doomed.

"The goal isn't to win by killing Recruiters or liberating the planet, because freedom is overrated. Its meaning will change for all earthlings. Winning doesn't always come through weapons but through time, and that's what we'll do: we'll win time, because that's the only thing that can save us."

Everyone understood him clearly, despite his sarcastic tone.

Larks walked toward those who were still recovering, moving slowly but steadily. Meanwhile, Onruks stood paralyzed, watching the sun gleam on Agui's skin.

The king took Axel's enhancers and motioned for the blushing young Knolot to approach. Obediently, the Knolot moved closer and took the orphaned human by the waist. Finding some circuits, he activated the enhancers. They glowed with blue light, extending along Axel's spine up to his neck. Two strips then reached down, covering his arms and embedding themselves into his bones like leeches piercing the skin. The enhancers adhered painfully, but it was a pain Axel could endure.

The enhancements forced him to stand upright, and as the pain subsided, a newfound will and enthusiasm clouded his vision and judgment. He began knocking down trees with a single blow, a feat that unsettled the Knolots. They had to restrain his hands and feet to prevent him from revealing their location.

Later, the three humans and Agui donned Recruiter armor, which fit perfectly. The young Gelyant grew claws, her body bending like a lion ready to pounce. The once-courageous humans now stood as armed warriors, their strength amplified, their hearts burning with resolve. They were covered with weapons from head to toe —bazookas, rifles, pistols, and powerful energy rays. This was their understanding of warfare and danger.

The group gathered to listen as Larks outlined the plan. Within his mind burned the spirit of revolution and an unquenchable thirst for vengeance against Perfidius.

EDIQUID